The Ups & Downs
OF A WOMAN'S
HEART

JENNA LEE SERIES BOOK 1

SONNY D. STONE

Publishing Coordinator – Sharon Kizziah-Holmes
Cover Design – Jaycee DeLorenzo

INDIE
PUB
PRESS

an imprint of A & S Publishing
A & S Holmes, Inc.

ISBN -13: 978-1-951772-73-4

Dedication

Special dedication to Sharon Stone, you are my fun loving rock. Jackie and Greg, you two inspire me daily. Steve and Stan, thanks for all the love and encouragement.

Acknowledgments

To my publishing coordinator who is supportive and patient, thank you, Sharon.

Heartfelt thanks to STB for years of encouragement.

Character Map

The Jamison Clan
Head of the Jamisons: Mrs. Ruth Jamison, (Grandma)

Six Sons: Adam, Charles, Francis, Darren, Everette and Franklin

Eight Grandsons: Caleb, Perry, Lawrence, Clinton, Jacob, Andrew, Edward and Joseph

The Bilmont Ancestory
Head of the Bilmonts: Mrs. Dorothy Bilmont, (Granny)

Mr. William Bilmont, (Partner)

Four Children: Sharon, Elaine, Dwayne, and Thomas

Eight Grandsons: Jeffrey, Gregory, Shawn, Troy, Michael, Matthew, Stanley and Steven

One Granddaughter: Jenna

The following story is realistic fiction. Enjoy the Ups and Downs of Jenna's journey!

Chapter 1

Who is Jenna Lee?

My cell phone buzzed for the third time this morning. I was busy teaching twenty-six kindergarteners and never had an opportunity to check my phone. I wasn't supposed to take personal calls during my workday, but it was concerning that I kept hearing the buzzing. About twenty minutes later, my classroom phone rang, the principal was on the line.

"Jenna, I have a substitute teacher walking to your classroom as we speak. Once you get her situated, I need you to get your purse and come to my office."

I hung up with more questions than when I answered. I met Mary at the door. "Students I have to leave early. This is Mrs. Tappmizer. Many of you have worked with her before." Mary, was a great friend and substitute teacher so I felt comfortable leaving my students in her care. I rushed down the hall to the office with my purse in hand and a very uneasy feeling in the pit of my stomach.

My mind is abuzz with questions. What in the world is going on that the principal would get me a substitute, tell me to get my stuff, and come to her office immediately? I don't think she's ever called me on my classroom phone before, much less gotten me a sub. I feel like I'm in big trouble, but I don't know why. My mind raced to figure out recent conversations I'd had with kids, teachers, and parents the last couple of days. Nothing of consequence came to mind and now I'm at her office door and I've got nothing, I'm absolutely blank. Am I being fired for something?

The principal stood, a forced, sorrowful looking grin on her face. She motioned for me come inside and have a seat. I stepped inside as she shut the door behind me. This is never a good sign, no matter how old you are. The principal shutting the door behind you means an intense conversation is about to occur. I glanced at the office secretary for help, but she just smiled a kind smile as the door shut. I felt a rush of anxiousness and nausea at the same time and knew whatever she was about to tell me was serious; something is very wrong. I'm being accused of something awful or someone I love must be hurt or dead. What could it be? I could feel my palms starting to sweat and my breathing increased. Mrs. Drake didn't sit behind her desk like usual. Instead she moved to the chair next to me, sat down at her round table, and finally started her dialogue.

She spoke in a soft gentle voice, "Jenna, I'm really sorry to have to tell you this but, I received a call from your brother Jeff, about an hour ago."

She had my full and undivided attention. I moved closer to her so I could hear every word. My brother is a very busy man, and if he called my school, this is a very serious situation. I tried to calm myself down so that I didn't get emotional and embarrass myself in front of my boss.

"He said he'd tried to reach you several times today on your cell but couldn't get hold of you. He felt he had no other option than to call our school and ask to speak to me. Your brother faxed you a plane ticket for the next flight out to see your Grandpa. I think he called him 'Partner'. Anyway, the report shared is that your Partner is not expected to live the next forty-eight hours. Your mom probably left you phone messages too, but your brother said she is already with your Grandma and Grandpa at their Kentucky home."

My mind was racing. I knew Partner seemed to be slipping but something must have happened for this swift decline. Poor Granny. *Focus Jenna listen to your boss, she's still talking.* I heard the principal saying my name. *I've got to pay attention and stay with the conversation.*

"The school secretary is the only other person at school who knows of your situation and she has volunteered to take care of your dogs while you are gone. She offered to take them to her house while you're away or will go to your house. Whatever you want, she just wanted to help."

What a sweetheart Ms. Leanne is to ease my mind and help me out in this stressful time. Leanne had been to my house several times and the dogs knew and liked her, so I felt very thankful for her friendship and kindness. I couldn't think for a minute, everything was happening so fast. I thanked Mrs. Drake for taking care of my class and getting my substitute.

"Jenna do whatever you need to do for your family and don't worry about work while you're gone. With your lesson plans in place, I'm sure Mrs. Tappmizer will do a great job while you are away. We can help if she has questions. Here's the faxed plane ticket from your brother. Jenna, if you need anything just text me or email me and I'll do what I can for you. So sorry you are dealing with this but it sounds like your family will be there to support one another."

"Thanks Mrs. Drake. I appreciate all you've done for me. I feel a little overwhelmed but will keep in touch."

I looked at the plane ticket in my hand and noticed I still had three hours before I had to be at the airport just thirty minutes away. I went back into my classroom and re-wrote detailed lesson plans for Mrs. Tappmizer. I wrote plans for the rest of the week and for the following week, just in case I'd have to stay at Partner and Granny's for an extended amount of time. I love my kindergarten kids, and I didn't want them to miss out on learning because I was going to be away. I explained my situation to Mary, and she indicated she had a clear schedule and could cover for me the entire time I needed to be gone. She offered to take care of my dogs too, but I told her Ms. Leanne had already volunteered. It's so wonderful to have great friends especially when life throws you unexpected curves.

I drove home and quickly grabbed several changes of clothes, shoes, and other necessary items into my suitcase. I tried to think of anything else I should bring and decided I might want a pair of comfy sweats to wear while I'm sitting around in the evening or at a hospital if that's where things evolved. I fed my two puppies, gave my four-legged fur balls good-bye hugs and kisses, and drove straight to the airport.

At the airport waiting to board my plane, I started to laugh. I can't believe I thought I was being fired. You hear terrible stories all the time about teachers being let go. I needed to clear my mind.

"Hey Jeff, this is your appreciative sister. What are you doing?"

"I'm on a plane headed to see Partner. Did you get the ticket I sent you?"

"Yes. I'm at the airport now. Just wanted to connect with you on when I'll be there."

"Sweetie, I bought the ticket for you, I know what flight, what time, and at what airport."

How could I be so spacey not to realize all of that before I called him? How embarrassing!

"Guess I'm a little off my game today bro. Thank you for the ticket and I'll meet you at the luggage pick-up."

"I've already made arrangements to get a rental car big enough for us and all your luggage. The stewardess is starting the turn off your electronic device speech, so I'll see you soon."

"Okay, love you."

"I should get there about an hour before you land. I'll meet you at the luggage carousal. Love you too, bye."

I finally took a deep breath to relax before boarding my plane.

My brother is two years older than me. He had always been very protective and caring of his little sister. Oh, don't think he's angelic by any means. Jeff is completely ornery, has a highly developed sense of humor, very intelligent, and has a well-balanced common sense about him that I love and adore.

My brother and I are very close. He's been my best friend ever since my first kindergarten memory. I got pushed down getting off the school bus on the first day of kindergarten. Jeff rushed to my side in the blink of an eye and yelled at the kid in front of all the other kids getting off the bus. Jeff, being older and intimidating, I thought he was going to hit that kid. But that mean little boy wet his pants in front of all the other kids. Jeff felt bad about that, but he walked me into my classroom. Then he walked the little boy to the office to get a change of clothes and to cheer him up for his first day of school.

Meanwhile, I forgot about my two bleeding knees, skinned up palms, ripped knees in my new red tights, and scuffed up new red shoes. I just stood up straight and tall and had a great first day of kindergarten. I even made friends with that little boy, Richie Johnston, before we got on the bus to go home that day. (Richie actually ended up being my first boyfriend, but that's an entirely different story and didn't happen until third grade.)

I had a new confidence knowing Jeff was going to be at my school to help me if I needed him. That's how I grew up, feeling safe and secure from all alarms. Jeff may have been a butthead at home as brothers can sometimes be, but in public he treated me like gold. He set the expectation of how to treat me and all followed his lead. I will admit I was spoiled and loved it growing up. Being the only girl rocked! I have several cousins and they are all boys, so I was admittedly a little princess.

Jeff has always been a good-looking kid and a handsome man for that matter (just don't tell him I admitted that). He grew up all farm boy. You know the type, riding, no actually racing horses, president of Future Farmers of America, quarterback football star and yes, the King at his junior and senior proms. He was very funny and had lots of friends over all the time. Pretty much the entire football team was at our house when they weren't on the field.

Another reason for all the boys at my house was because my mom is the best cook and loves to bake. Seriously, homemade food from scratch, apple dumplings, pies, cinnamon rolls. What a great memory, having a house full of young people, laughter, and tons of food. I'm making myself hungry. I need to think about something else.

Chapter 2

The Flight

Since my ticket was bought at the last minute, I was stuck in the middle seat for an hour non-stop flight between two large-sized men. I felt like a "squished sandwich". One, a middle-aged man in a dark brown suit; the other younger, I'd guess late twenties, good looking, and dressed like a rap music hip-hop star. The suit man was polite, said "hello", quietly sat by the window and started working on his laptop. The hipster, in the aisle seat, would not stop talking to me. At first it was kind of cool hearing him talking in rhythm with every phrase he spoke. He seemed nice enough, but seriously, he talked non-stop from the moment I found my seat. Usually people take a breath, but this guy was constant chatter. If I looked away from him, he physically tapped me; once on the leg and once on my shoulder to get my full attention. I felt trapped, like I was being held hostage.

I got situated with my seatbelt on, only physically

touching the "suit man", and praying this other man would give me a break with the noise. But just before take-off, the stewardess came up and told me I'd been upgraded to first class. I think I actually jumped over the hip-hop man to get into the aisle. I couldn't believe I was being upgraded, but I thought God had seen my need and worked a miracle to get away from "the non-stop rapper". I smiled and almost hugged her. "Thank you for upgrading me."

With a very matter of fact tone and facial expression the attendant replied, "I had nothing to do with the seating change." Confused, I followed stewardess Kristi, as her name tag designated, to the front of the plane. I quickly saw why I received the sudden and much needed upgrade.

"Ms. Lee, this handsome man just paid to have you upgraded to first class. I'm guessing you will want to sit next to him. I'll make the arrangements.

I looked and was surprised to see my cousin Greg sitting in seat 5C. We are very close, more like brother and sister the way we kid around with each other. When I was very young, I couldn't say "Greg". For some reason, it came out "Gig" and it sort of stuck. I think I'm the only one who still calls him that on occasion, but he lets it slide because it's me, his favorite and only girl cousin. I don't know why he doesn't think it's as cute as I think it is. Maybe it's a manhood thing.

"Gig, oh my gosh, what in the world are you doing here?" Nicknames from childhood stick sometimes. "I mean, Greg. I'm so glad you are here, and thank you!"

"I'm flying to see Partner too. I was in town for a business meeting. But, the call about Partner changed my plans. Then on the plane when I saw you, in the middle of those two large men, I had to help you out of your seating situation. I think the young rapster is sweet on you Jenna. Did you see his face when you literally jumped over him to get away?"

"No, I didn't." I poked Greg in the arm, all the while

knowing he just spent a lot of money to make sure I was comfortable on this flight. Tell me I don't have a wonderful family!

I settled in to enjoy my first-class status. I don't know why the airlines can't make all the seats bigger and allow more leg room for all their paying customers. It's just the right thing to do. Also, they don't just give you one bag of pretzels in first class. You can have a variety of treats. I munched, crunched, and enjoyed my time with Greg. We laughed and caught up on things. My family, especially my cousins, are really hilarious! I think we have a genetic gift of innocently getting ourselves into the funniest situations. When I get tickled, I have a giggly girl laugh and others laugh when they hear me. I don't mind, I'm used to it. I noticed the first-class passengers laughing at us, even though they have no clue why we are laughing. It's great to know we can share the love. I figure the world needs more laughter, right?

The flight literally flew by and Greg and I headed to the luggage return area. I somehow got my two-inch heels caught on the carpet and went sailing across the room. I was running forward trying to catch my balance before my head banged into the wall. I threw both my hands out to stop myself. I slowly turned around hoping Greg did not see my "graceful" moment, but no such luck. He was doubled over laughing, tears running down his face. And sadly, he wasn't the only one who had seen my graceful moment. How embarrassing! I hate it when I'm so entertaining. Me in high heels... not a good mix. I've always heard if you dress nice you might get upgraded if the airline overbooks the flight. I love my pink pumps. but I only wear them when I want to wow someone. I guess this was a wow moment, just not the same wow factor I was going for.

We reached the luggage carousal and Greg got his

luggage but my luggage was nowhere to be found. Just my luck. Apparently, the non-stop flight didn't load my luggage on my plane before we left. The airport representative said they will shuttle it to me and I should have it within the next twenty-four to forty-eight hours. Great! I should have packed clean underwear and a toothbrush in my purse. If I hadn't been so rushed to come see Partner, I would have thought about things like that. After filling out the paperwork to have my luggage forwarded to Granny's house, Greg and I met Jeff at the luggage return and all of us rode together in Jeff's rental to Granny's house. Greg couldn't wait to tell Jeff about my graceful promenade across the airport floor. All I heard was, "...her long legs in those pink high heels were flying across the floor," and they were both cracking up.

Greg is a year younger than Jeff, and on the way to Partner's they talked frenziedly. Usually I'm pretty talkative but with the two of them in the same place, it was way more entertaining to just sit back and listen. They are both so humorous trying to outdo each other with their stories and they are so animated with their hand gestures and facial expressions. I just sat in the back seat and laughed so hard I cried. I'll be honest they had to pull over once for me to use the restroom because I was laughing so hard. I knew we had a somber time ahead of us with Partner and Granny, so the comic relief was welcomed and appreciated.

Granny never wants to be called "Grandma" because she thinks the title is for old women. So, she wants her grandchildren to call her "Granny". Personally, I always thought Granny sounds like an older term of endearment than Grandma, but it was what I grew up with so that's what we all call her. Partner got his nickname from Jeff.

Jeff, being the oldest grandchild, would visit Grandpa as a toddler when he was learning to walk and talk. Grandpa would greet Jeff by saying, "Hey, Partner, how you doing, little man?"

Jeff would respond, "Hi, Partner". Then Partner would take his pointer finger and aim it at Jeff like a gun and pull back the thumb. Jeff would do it right back at him. Partner would laugh every time and Jeff loved the attention even at an early age. As Jeff got older it just got shortened; Partner this, Partner that, and the rest of us cousins grew up addressing him as our one and only "Partner."

Granny and Partner have four children, two girls and two boys. We have lots of first cousins and with the internet and Facebook we've all remained close even though we live all over the country.

It is sad to say, but everyone is so busy with our own lives that we don't really all get together unless it's a hospital situation or funeral. I realized we need to get together for something positive and decided to work on a family reunion after all this is over. It would have to be in Kentucky because Granny will never travel away from Partner and their farm. I'll check into getting that organized maybe this summer. If this is going to happen, it will be up to me. Past experience has taught me we will talk about wanting to do it, but it will never happen. Great, another thing to add to my "to-do list".

Finally, we arrived at Granny and Partner's driveway, which was already full of cars. I love the memories of pulling off the highway and driving onto their gravel road. As a child, that was my clue we were close to Partner and Granny's. I knew it was time to wake up from our long drive. Growing up we didn't have Bluetooth or DVD players in cars. We had the radio, CDs, and each other. Jeff and I would be arguing before we got out of town and my mom or dad, if he was with us, would threaten to pull over the car and spank us both if we didn't settle down.

Road trips to Partner's always involved lots of music. We'd practice our three or four-part harmony with different songs from the radio, usually country stations. By the time we got to Granny's, we were all feeling pretty happy to be working together making beautiful music. We'd have snacks in the car, but I'd always needed to stop to use the restroom.

Dad didn't like to make unnecessary stops, he wanted to get where he was headed as soon as possible. I think it was some male bragging right to say, "I drove hundreds of miles in such and such a time." With this being the case, I would tell dad I had to use the restroom whenever I had the slightest inkling, because it would take him many miles and several exits and towns before he would finally pull over to let me go. I remember embarrassing times when dad was driving, and it was an emergency bathroom stop where I had to squat by the road and go. But thank goodness that didn't happen very often.

My grandparents lived in a large home that Partner built when they first got married. They have lived in it over fifty years and updated and added on to the house. The large white pillars out front and the wrap-around porch was a favorite part of Partner's Kentucky home. Miles and miles of white fences contrasted against the deep, beautiful, green grassy fields and hills. And there were horses enough for all of us kids to ride and then some.

I love my country memories at Partner and Granny's. But this trip is for Partner and the here and now. As we hit his driveway I just wanted to get inside the house, see him, and make sure he is okay. I just want to let him know I am here for him. I needed to give my mom a hug and tell her I love her. I'm sure this is hard for her to watch the process of losing her dad.

Chapter 3

Granny and Partner's

My granny is old-fashioned in every way. She thinks she dressed nice, but she only buys something if it is on sale or at a garage sale. It's not like she couldn't afford to buy new things, she just refuses to pay full price for things, especially for herself. She is always clean but in a style several seasons past. I always tried to style Granny with something new, but she would just write me a letter telling me I shouldn't waste my money. The worst part is she would never wear what I got her. She says she is saving such nice clothes for something special. I think she just feels better in her bargain clothes, so I finally stopped. I see her in her flowery dresses and old lady shoes and know that's my Granny's comfort zone.

She also didn't like doctors, she never did. When any doctor gave her advice for Partner or herself, she would decide if she agreed with them or not. If she thought she knew better, she would do what she wanted to do, no matter what. Even though Granny had no formal medical training. We would ask her where she got her premise for her opinion and she would say "I bought a health book from a garage sale." Who knows how old it was. She would always say doctors' "practice" and they don't really know anyway.

With Granny's aversion to doctors and a deep seeded distrust of any kind of medication, my family worked very hard and long to help Granny see Partner's deterioration and his growing need for Hospice care for his final days. Let me just say that my mom and her siblings had to do a lot of talking to convince Granny. They basically said Grandpa would either have to go to the hospital or he could stay home with Hospice. In her mind she picked the lesser of two evils.

Granny thinks she can still take care of Partner like she did when she was younger, but her grasp on reality is somewhat diminished now as well. Granny believes no one can do things as good as she can. Or as she says, the "right way". It's Granny's way of doing things, or the highway because she's older and knows all, like Yoda from Star Wars, only she has no idea who that is. If you'd ask her "why" she'd immediately respond, "Because I said so, that's why." There was no discussion with Granny. You just listened. Grandma should have been a preacher because she reads the Bible all the time and would quote scriptures when you were trying to have a conversation. And with Granny and God on one side and you on the other, like I said, it was a moot point. Granny wins, and you lose every time.

After continuous efforts by all her children individually and as a group, she couldn't change any of her kids' minds, so she finally let the Hospice nurses help in her home with Partner's last days of care. They assured Granny it would just be a couple days at most.

I have a great respect for Hospice care personnel. It's a great in-home program for people who need help when there are no medical cures available. The nurses who helped Partner were kind and friendly not just with Partner but with Granny and our entire family.

All four of Granny's kids are by Partner's bedside, Mom (Sharon), Elaine, Dwayne, and Thomas. Mom wants to know if I want to see Partner to say a final goodbye. My mind flashed back instantly to just a year earlier when I stood next to my dad's hospital bedside and watched him take his last breath of life. This is a picture that never really leaves your heart or the back of your mind. I didn't know if I want or could handle another picture like that in my mind playing over and over in my memory, but I knew I had to see Partner alive at least one more time to say good-bye. I want him to know I am here for him and remind him that I love him.

I walked into the bedroom and Partner is in his bed struggling for each labored breath. He is in great distress and what is just as horrifying are the looks on the faces of his kids watching him suffer with each breath. It rips my heart into pieces. I won't let myself be weak and cry, I have to be here for a reason. Jeff and I looked at each other and knew we had to help Partner and our mom, aunt, and uncles with this morbid scene. After each of us saying silent prayers and all of us just watching him in his bed, it became too crowded in that room. I wanted to get some fresh air, but the timing isn't right yet.

I did however walk out of the room with Granny following at my heels. I took a hold of her hand and said, "Granny, the Hospice nurse can administer morphine to Partner and that will help him leave this world with ease and comfort, not struggling for each and every breath. Jeff and I had the nurses do this for my dad and he left this life peacefully." Granny said she'd think about it. After much discussion, and with everyone in the home being of the same opinion to ease Partner's pain and agony, Granny reluctantly agreed to try the medicine and see if it helped him.

Once the nurse administered the morphine Partner began breathing comfortably almost immediately, and quite honestly so did the rest of us. It was like we all collectively began to breath comfortably once Partner wasn't struggling with his breathing anymore. Granny saw the big difference the medicine made for Partner. She would never admit it, but we all knew she felt better about her decision. With Partner resting peacefully, and a room and house full of people waiting for death, I really needed to step outside and get some fresh air for myself.

Partner was once a strong businessman, hard-working and well respected. Now he has shrunk down to a small frail looking man. His eyes are sunken in and glazed over with a milky haze, but those blue eyes are still as blue as ever. I'm sure he doesn't even know who I am at this point.

I am here for my Partner, Granny, my mom, and family. I don't want to focus on Partner in his diminished condition, instead I choose to remember the pictures in my mind of him in healthier days when we played horseshoes at his horseshoe pit he created. He relaxed by throwing horseshoes and enjoyed beating anyone who would get into the pit with him. I remember the loud belly-rolling laughs when he was beating me every time. He is a real man's man and worked hard at everything he did. He has a great sense of humor and loves God, family, music, and making others feel valued.

As I am breathing in a deep breath of fresh Kentucky air, I can also remember Partner singing around a campfire and making s'mores, or one of the canoe trips we took when all the cousins and family got together and floated down the river. Wonderful times of fun, laughter, and love. That's what I'm going to think about, not the gurgling sounds of death coming to take Partner away. As my mind flooded with memories of Partner, I decided to take a short walk in this fresh Kentucky air. I'd been sitting on an airplane, and sitting in the house. A nice walk would be refreshing and help clear my mind.

Jeff strolled out on the porch to make sure I am okay. I told him I'm fine and thinking about walking down the road over to Granny's neighbors before it gets dark, to let them know about Partner's condition. They had been neighbors for around forty-five years. Their home is a mansion compared to Partner and Granny's house. Although with six bedrooms and four baths Partner's house is nothing to sneeze at. Out in the country against miles and miles of land, it's easy for a house to look small, but Granny and Partner's house always felt just right, not too big, and not too small.

Granny had more of a minimalistic feel to her home. Always warm and inviting but not full of clutter like some old ladies' homes. I love that about her. I've cleaned houses for older ladies before to earn extra cash and the clutter can be unbelievable. Tiny collectables covered in dust and collections of dolls sitting all over beds. It was just too much for me. Anyway, Granny has plenty of bedrooms. However, when the situation presented itself for us all to be at Granny and Partner's like now, we all end up sleeping on the floor in the living room by the huge round stone fireplace; so we won't miss out on anything and we can stay up together and talk. We have great times in that old house, lots of love, laughter, and music.

I reminded Jeff I was taking my phone with me and to call if anything changes with Partner. I had second thoughts about leaving the house. I feel like part of me wants a break from the house of stress, to get some fresh air, but part of me doesn't want to leave the comfort and familiarity of the old farmhouse. I often feel an inward struggle of what I want to do and what I should do. I guess I don't have a poker face because Jeff put his arm around me with a reassuring smile.

"Partner's condition could take a while yet, so go ahead and get some fresh air. I'm here, Greg, Shawn, and Matt are here covering phones and airport runs if needed. Mom and the siblings have help if they want or need it. Go over to Ms. Ruth's house for a while and tell her I said hello. Do you want some company on your walk, or just some alone time?"

"If you're sure it will be okay with everyone, I won't be long. I could use the alone time, to process things. Thanks." Walking down a rock road in high heels is not easy, especially for a klutz like me. I would have changed into my tennis shoes, but no luggage. I almost took off my shoes and walked in the grass by the side of the road but was afraid I'd step on something that would injure my feet. I considered going back to Granny's house and asking to borrow her shoes but didn't want to add to her plate. So, I walked on slowly and carefully on the balls of my feet. It took me longer than I anticipated to make the mile down the curvy road. I looked up and saw Ms. Ruth's beautiful house just as the road comes to a final turn. I knew I could make it the rest of the way with my shoes on protecting my feet.

The neighbor lady, Ms. Ruth, is Granny's age, and she has six sons. She owns a vast expanse of land including a large horse ranch with lots of hired hands. She is very business minded and I've never heard her lose a debate or an argument. She is one tough lady. I always liked her and as a child I would sneak over to see her and her horses when I visited my grandparents. She was always very pretty, slender and petite in frame, and in contrast to my Granny always dressed in the latest hair and clothing styles.

Each summer every grandchild would spend a week or two at Partners until we got older and our summer schedules filled up with sports and jobs. During my childhood summer visits, Ms. Ruth would invite me over to her house and let me drink coffee with her like a grown-up. I love coffee to this day and think it's all her fault.

Granny never liked me going to see Ms. Ruth. Ms. Ruth isn't a church going woman and therefore a bad influence on me. According to Granny, Ms. Ruth wears uppity clothes, is ruthless and thinks she's better than everyone else. Granny heard through small town gossip that she drinks and smokes. Granny was always mad at Partner when I let it slip that he and I have gone over to see Ms. Ruth. I'd always feel bad about it and Partner would just wink at me like he was telling me "that's okay, Jenna". I know my Granny wouldn't let it go and I am sure after I left, Partner got an earful all because I can't keep a secret. I'm really not a fan of keeping secrets.

As I reached the front door, one of Ms. Ruth's handsome grandsons greeted me with a knockout smile. I introduced myself. He escorted me into the parlor to wait for Ms. Ruth. While I waited, four more men about my age entered the room. I didn't remember their names, but I recognized them from younger years. They were all Ruth's grandsons, and all have their Grandma's beautiful blue eyes. Wow, I feel like I am in a candy shop and I need to run out quick before all those calories stick to me! How is it possible to have all these great looking men in one location? *Did I fall and hit my head? Am I in heaven?* My inner monologue is distracting me from my current surroundings.

These handsome men all have varying shades of sun-bleached blond hair and their arms are like fitness magazine models. I guess these men do a lot of lifting bales of hay or something heavy. I had a sudden and strong urge to go squeeze their arms and hold on all the way up to their broad shoulders. They are all standing here like they are ready for a photo shoot in wrangler blue jeans, white tee-shirts under a partly unbuttoned shirt, and cowboy boots. There is way too much handsome in one room for me to feel comfortable. I am not used to being around one handsome man, much less a whole group. I loved the undivided attention when they started flirting with me, until the boys redirected our conversation back to my childhood days. The men reminding me of stupid stuff we did together as kids. The laughter in the room was infectious.

"Hey, Jenna, do you remember the time we were teaching you to ride a horse bareback and the horse kicked to shoo a fly away? You lost your balance, fell off the horse, and fell into a pile of horse manure." The boys were laughing and staring at me in hopes they could hear my response over the roar of their laughter.

"Yeah, I remember something like that." My life seemed to have many of those moments. The kind that others laugh at for years and you can still see the picture clearly in your mind like it was yesterday. Yeah that's got me written all over it.

Finally, the boys' boisterous laughter quieted, and I saw Ms. Ruth enter the room. She moved a little slower than I remembered. All the men stood a little taller and their laughter stopped almost in unison the moment she entered the room. They stepped back in a straight line against the beautiful wooden wall as she walked over to personally welcome me to her home.

Chapter 4

Ms. Ruth

I hugged her and she felt smaller than I remembered. She has a full head of beautiful white hair, and her eyes are still as crystal blue as I remembered. She sat with perfect posture and invited me to sit next to her. The boys just stood against the wall and watched us. I couldn't figure out why these men were just standing around staring at us? Don't they have jobs in the middle of the day? Where are their wives or girlfriends? Hot guys like that don't just stand around for my viewing pleasure. Girls I know are texting, sexting, and talking about texting and sexting men like these. I feel like I've been given a precious gift if only for a few short minutes, so I just needed to smile and enjoy the scenery. *Would it be too much to ask them if I can take a picture?* Maybe it's jetlag, or stress that Partner is dying, but these men were very impressive individually. Together, they were overpowering masculine and I was doing everything in my power not to stare, drool, or trip over my own feet. This is always a real concern for me in the presence of the opposite sex.

Ms. Ruth invited me to sit for a cup of coffee and I couldn't refuse her for old time sake. It was just what I needed actually. I love my coffee. Ms. Ruth isn't the talkative type but when she says something it has meaning.

"Jenna, darling, it looks like you are taking good care of yourself and you finally lost those extra pounds you carried for so long."

"Thank you, Ms. Ruth." *Nice to sneak in a dig about me being a fat kid in front of these hot men.* I am doing great. I came to be with Partner, his health is failing, and he isn't long for this world."

Partner has always been a big flirt, and he never meets a stranger he doesn't consider a new friend. Male or female, young or old, animal or human, he could make friends with anyone; he is the kindest man I've ever known. He isn't a fake kind of nice, he is the real deal. I never heard him say one unkind word, to anyone ever. And not to knock a girl when she's down but living with my Granny, that's saying something for Partner.

Partner always enjoys visiting with Ms. Ruth. Any occasion he can find to head down the road to see her, he's on his horse riding across the pasture to her farm.

I think he secretly had a crush on Ms. Ruth. She is very pretty, even as an older woman. But in my memory of her younger days, she was outright movie star stunning. Partner would never overstep the neighbor's line of appropriateness, but when he isn't working, he is visiting with someone somewhere. It would make Granny so mad. She didn't have cell phones back in their younger days, so she knew if she couldn't locate him, he was off visiting with someone and he'd be home when he was finished talking with his new or old friends.

Like I mentioned earlier, Granny is not fond of Ms. Ruth, and that's been as far back as I can remember. She was never encouraging when we wanted to go outside and play with Ms. Ruth's grandsons, the Jamison boys, when we were here for summer stays. But we always found a time, always with Partner, to make it over to her farm.

I think both Granny and Ms. Ruth are very strong-willed women. Stubbornness might be an attribute or skill women of their day needed to achieve great things. Partner would never ever have an affair on Granny, he was old school that way, but that didn't stop him from going out of his way to make women feel special. He would always find a way to compliment a woman on how pretty her hair, or dress, or smile were. If a woman entered a room, he would stand in respect. I love that old-fashioned respect men used to show women. Some men still do, I'm not slamming men, just saying… I like it.

Women and men of Granny's era and generation were physically hard-working people. They had to be to survive. The women of Ms. Ruth's and Granny's day supported their families starting out with practically nothing and saved and worked and cooked and sewed and sacrificed to accomplish great things for their families. They did it all from scratch, it inspires me to meet men and women of that era and hear their life stories. It makes me all the more thankful for the microwaves, washing machines, cars, cell phones, computers and other great inventions I enjoy today. Well enough for my nostalgia moment.

"Ms. Ruth, I can't stay long." The boys, Andrew, Perry, Edward, and Joey all made a loud exhale sound together. It made me jump. I'd forgotten they were all still there staring at us. I smiled but Ms. Ruth just gave them a stern look. Not exactly a frown, but the eyes definitely let them know they interrupted and that was unsatisfactory with her.

Me being me, finally had to voice my curiosity. "I'm sorry, Ms. Ruth, but can you tell me why these handsome men are inside on this beautiful day?"

Ms. Ruth responded mono-toned, "My grandsons work

for me. We just had a staff meeting. They do what I say, and go where I want them to go, when I want them to go."

Ms. Ruth owns lots of land, stock, and makes wise business investments. She has great power and a steely coldness to her tone that I hadn't known or remembered as a child. "Ms. Ruth, I'm sorry if I interrupted a meeting or something important. I really should be going but just couldn't be this close to you and not stop by to say hello. Oh, I almost forgot, Jeff asked me to be sure and send his best to you and your family as well."

"How long are you planning on staying?"

"It depends on how Partner progresses. Most of the family is already here or on their way to the farm as we speak

"Sorry to hear about your Partner's condition. He's always been a great man in our community, a great neighbor, and a personally close friend. He will be missed. If you need anything, all you have to do is ask, you know that."

That's when I heard him, cowboy boots walking in on the wooden porch, with a smooth and steady gate. He was whistling a tune to a county song I'd heard before but couldn't remember the name of. Then I heard the sound of the screen door slamming shut behind him. He strolled inside with six packs, one in each hand and spoke in a low jovial tone as he announced, "Howdy, bros, it's five o'clock! You can have your own lives for a few hours and then back to Ms... Oh, I'm sorry Grandma! I didn't know you had company. I didn't see a car in the driveway. I apologize for my interruption."

Ms. Ruth responded in a non-emotional affect, but with a disapproving glare, "Jacob, this is Mr. Belmont's granddaughter, Jenna. You may remember her from her visits as a child."

I said "hello" to him in a quieter voice than I had planned on. He was off the charts gorgeous; what is his name again, isn't it Jace, Jacoby, Jacob? *Think Jenna think and listen.* He was movie star pinup eye-candy handsome and then some. He was tall. I'm guessing 6'4ish, sporting his thick, dark, slightly wavy hair, blue eyes as crystal as an ocean, and broad shoulders. He wore wrangler jeans, and a white button-down shirt, with the sleeves folded a couple of cuff links off his strong manly wrists.

I immediately looked at his hand for a wedding ring and saw nothing there. But some of these cowboy types don't wear rings, because it could get caught in ropes, machines, etc. So that really isn't a good indicator of his availability or not...

It suddenly got very warm in Ms. Ruth's living room. The boys quickly walked up to Jacob and freed him of the beers. They were all smiles, each taking a beer in one hand and hitting each other in the upper arm with the other fist. Ms. Ruth did not look happy to see alcohol in her home, or her boys acting so giddy.

She and my Granny never approved of their families drinking alcohol. Ms. Ruth didn't want her boys acting out, and Granny felt that alcohol was the root of all evil. She would say "Alcohol is a tool of the devil. It will cause you to lose your ability to think clearly and make bad choices instead of good ones. It only takes one bad choice to ruin your future." She may not have been too far off on the evils of alcohol, but my generation likes alcohol. It's the social drug of choice. Things were always black or white with Granny, never any room for gray. She'd call gray areas compromise and that was border line evil in her thinking too. Right is right, wrong is wrong.

Ms. Ruth is known to cuss every now and then and drinks on occasion, but she doesn't want her boys doing that because they aren't as strong as her in her powerful opinion. She is sure she could manage a slip of the tongue every now and then and a few drinks every once in a while, but she doesn't think her boys should drink or use foul language in public. It wouldn't look good for their family name. Family and reputation were everything.

My Granny on the other hand would wash your mouth out with soap if you said the word "butt" or "fart" in earshot of her. Needless to say, no one says anything like that around my Granny. I've had firsthand experience of soap washings in my mouth and can I just say "YUCK!". Lava soap does not taste good. I can remember the horror of it to this day.

Nowadays' kids have legal rights and that would have been considered child abuse to force a child to wash their mouth out with dirty old hand soap. I didn't agree with her methods, however no one says questionable words around Granny even as adults. Mostly out of respect but partly out of fear.

Once I heard Jeff say "crap" within earshot of Granny. My cousins and I sitting there with him at the time, all took off running out the front door, for fear Granny heard and we'd all be in trouble. We had a good laugh, and the boys threatened Jeff if he didn't watch his language around Granny. Thank goodness her hearing isn't as good as it used to be with all of us getting together now. The boys try to watch their language out of respect for Granny when she's around. I think it's very sweet. We really don't need the foul language anyway, but somehow it creeps into our vocabulary and pops up at times of great stress. Working with kindergarteners every day, I pay close attention to my words and work on my off-time vocabulary to keep questionable words out of my mouth, so I don't slip and say them in front of a student.

Ruth spoke in a firm authoritative voice, bringing me back to attention. "You know how I feel about you drinking, boys. Not in my house!"

They all said "yes ma'am" in perfect unison. Then they all held the beers behind their backs while they stood there staring at me. I was shocked a woman of her age had so much power over these grown men. They couldn't even drink in front of her. Was it out of respect or fear? I couldn't tell. Maybe a little of both.

"Thank you, Ms. Ruth, for the coffee, it is good to see you again. I'm so glad you are in good health and are doing well with the farm and family."

"Jenna, are you still a teacher? Isn't it kindergarten?"

I was surprised she knew my career path. It had been years since I'd talked with Ms. Ruth. Partner must have told her. He loved to visit and brag on his grandchildren.

"Yes, and I love teaching."

"Are you seeing anyone?"

I noticed Jacob's right eyebrow rise like he was waiting for my response too. Was he interested in my dating status? Wishful thinking on my part.

"Not anyone special." The truth was, no one at all. But I would never admit that in this setting with all these great looking men staring at me. Think about it, who meets eligible men teaching five-year-olds all day long? I go out with girlfriends but not to "pick up guys".

I didn't feel comfortable with the questions coming my way, so I spoke up to lead the conversation in a different direction. "Ms. Ruth, it is great seeing you and the family again, but I need to get back to check on Partner and do what I can to help out. Thanks again for the coffee."

Jacob immediately stepped up to me and said, "I'll walk you home."

Chapter 5

Jacob

He reached out for my hand and without thinking I reached out for his too. His hand was large, strong, and rugged compared to mine. He leaned down to my ear and in a gentle low whisper said, "Your hand is so soft, Jenna."

I thought how can you tell with your rough hand? But thank God I didn't say that out loud. For once I kept my mouth shut. I just smiled up at him and said, "Thanks."

And there was something else. The way he said my name. I couldn't put my finger on it, but I liked it. It was almost soothing to me deep inside. Like he tickled the inside of my stomach; the weirdest sensation I'd ever felt before. My neck had goose bumps where his warm, sweet breath touched me.

As we walked out onto the deck of the house, all the brothers followed us out the door, now with their beers in front of them. He asked if I had time for a swing before I went back to Grandpa's house. The Jamison's had an old tree swing at the back of the house that we used to swing on as kids. I'd forgotten all about it.

"I'd love to swing but I have to make it quick." As we walked around the back of the house, the brothers followed along the porch watching our every step. It was really starting to get creepy having an audience. I couldn't take it any longer, I had to say something.

"So, what's the deal with your brothers? I feel like I'm their entertainment side show, Jacob. Where are their girlfriends and wives?"

He laughed out loud.

"What's so funny?"

"Grandma Ruth has high standards for her family and to be totally honest, no woman has ever been good enough for any of her boys. They are falling all over themselves, because for some reason, she likes you. They must be in shock because they've never seen her approve of another woman before, ever. That's why they are studying you so intently."

"What do you mean for some reason? Jacob, don't you know, I am terrific!"

In the sexiest tone I've ever heard, he said with a low tender voice, "Yeah, I'm noticing that about you."

"Ha ha, Jacob." I was uncomfortable with my poor attempt at humor and him talking about me, so I quickly changed the subject. I was proud of myself that I could think so quickly when I was so smitten by Jacob's good looks.

"You brought in alcohol for your brothers and your Grandma was not pleased about your behavior. You must be the bad boy in the family. Do you live on the ranch?"

"No, my brothers all live on her 3,500 acres, but I have my own businesses, my own land, my own place, my own life."

"Do you have a wife and or kids?"

"No."

"Really I would have guessed…. Wait, why not?"

"I guess I never met the right one for me."

"That's too bad; because you're…." I stopped talking. I couldn't believe I said that much out loud. I was thinking how mind blowing hot he is, but my mouth started talking before my brain could turn off my mouth.

He smiled and said, "Yes, you were saying?" The smirk on his face was adorable.

I blushed and tried to change the subject yet again. "Hey, your brothers are all watching. Should I ask one of them to push me on this old tree swing, or can you handle it?"

His eyes burned through me like hot coals from a fire, and then for a second time he used a voice as sexy as I had ever heard. "Oh I can handle it."

I felt hot and embarrassed again, so I quickly sat my butt on the wooden swing. This old swing was a great memory from my childhood. It brought back times when we were catching fireflies, squeezing the lit-up part and writing our names on our shirts with the bug bottoms so it would glow in the dark. It was great fun. We also played freeze tag, rode horses, fished, and went swimming in their huge lake in the moonlight.

My mind moved back to the here and now. The first push on the old tree swing involved Jacob's fingers brushing strongly against my jean pockets and I had tingles all over my body.

Good grief, what is wrong with me? This man is good looking, okay better than good looking, but my body is going to putty at a mere graze from his finger. His deep, low voice commanded my attention, yet a gentle kindness to his tone did something to my insides. I could listen to him talk for hours. Reality Jenna, you need to get back to Partner's.

"Jacob, that's enough, I really should go."

"Jacob, stop daydreaming back there, I need to go dude."

He moved around in front of the swing and held both sides of the swing ropes throwing my body out so quickly that I practically landed on his feet. I didn't fall because his arm was now around my lower back to steady me.

He smelled wonderful up close. Like an outdoors man, sort of a mix between newly cut grass and a faint musky smell. Both mixed with just out of the dryer fresh sheets smell. I don't know how long we stood this close, but he brought me back to attention when he said, "If you are going to stand this close to me, I'm going to have to kiss you."

My sassy side kicked in and I retorted, "Is it because your brothers are waiting on the sidelines for a show?"

"No, because if I don't kiss you, I'll always wonder what it would have been like and my imagination is very vivid, so I might as well lay one on you."

I blushed at his honesty. "Jacob, you aren't missing anything. I'm not a good kisser."

"I doubt that." He squeezed his arm around my waist and pulled me the short distance we were apart. Our bodies were full on touching each other from head to toe. He leaned his head back away from my face so he could look into my eyes and paused, not moving, just breathing deeply and staring into my eyes. I couldn't feel my legs. I lost all strength to stand on my own. My entire body was one pulsing reaction to his voice, his smell, his eyes, his strength holding me. *How could he have this kind of consuming power over me? I am seriously in unfamiliar water; this has never happened to me before. I've never felt this way about anyone, this is crazy!*

What would happen to me if he did kiss me? Frankly my dear, I didn't care, I had to kiss him. I had no will to deny him. I was mesmerized by him. He slid both his hands onto my butt cheeks and lifted me up to his waist.

I instinctively wrapped my legs around him tightly and our lips embraced. I had been married before and I'd never kissed my ex-husband this way. I'm not sure where my hands were, around his neck, in his hair, down his back, all three? I was absorbed in his arms, his mouth, his taste, his touch, his smell and I didn't want to be anywhere but in his arms. I don't know how much time passed, how many kisses, but the brothers were all staring. I had forgotten all about them until my cell phone vibrated, bringing me back to my senses. Jacob slowly placed me back down on my own two feet. I sort of stumbled back two steps before I could get strength enough to stand on my own two feet again. Jacob quickly had his hands on my shoulders to steady me.

Jeff texted I needed to head back to Partner's. He said he would come get me if I needed a ride.

"Jacob, I really need to get back to Partner's now."

"Let me drive you up the road."

"Thanks, I'd appreciate that. Let me text Jeff and let him know I'm on my way." Honestly, I didn't think my legs would work to walk me back to the house. My legs still felt like melted butter. Plus it was starting to get dark outside with storm clouds rolling in.

I looked in his sultry eyes. Jacob paused and grinned a schoolboy grin, then leaned into my ear, moved my hair away, and with his hot breath whispered, "Best first kiss ever Jenna."

My heart skipped a beat. I had goose bumps all up and down my neck where his whisper landed. All I could do was smile like a silly schoolgirl and say "yeah." I waved at the brothers and they just stared, no waves, no smiles, just stares. So creepy. I don't need creepy in my life. I need to be with my family, not out looking for hot men. But, oh dear Lord, Jacob was like my new favorite pair of jeans, comfortable, and a good fit.

During the truck ride to Partner's house, I was nervous

to be alone with such a man. So much had happened in such a short amount of time. I started talking about my brother. Jacob knew Jeff, so that's where my conversation naturally went, to what we had in common. And more importantly it wasn't making me think of kissing Jacob again. A safe topic, that he would be interested in and I could talk without having to think.

"My considerate brother knew I didn't have money for a ticket to come see Partner, so he made arrangements to get me one. He knew that if he would have asked me if I wanted to come and say goodbye to Partner, I would have told him no, just so he wouldn't spend his money on me. That's Jeff, always my amazingly great brother. He's really the best. I love him."

Even with all the conversation, my mind kept floating back to Jacob, our kiss, and if and when I could see him again. I clearly have been on my own, single, and lonely too long. It's not smart to let any man have so much of my attention so quickly. I have to protect myself so I don't get hurt. I feel like my heart has been in hibernation during a long winter season. Now Jacob has finally and suddenly brought me back to life. Wasn't there a fairy tale like that? Sleeping Beauty, I think? *No fairy tales Jenna, reality Jenna. You live in the here and now. Dreams like Jacob don't happen for me, snap out of it.*

We are in the driveway at Partner's in no time at all. Jacob hadn't said more than two words to me. That could be because I talked non-stop the entire trip. When I'm nervous I tend to talk to fill the silence and if I'm really, really nervous I talk really fast.

"Thank you for the ride, Jacob."

"I hope your Grandpa will be okay and if you need anything please let me know. I'd love to help anyway I can." Jacob leaned over and spoke softly, "Can I call you? I'd love to see you again. Your kiss did something to me, Jenna, you touched me." He gently placed his hand on my leg as he spoke. I could feel his heat and my heart was beating so hard I was sure he could feel my pulse in my leg.

I didn't know what to say, what did he mean, I touched him? Then my self-doubting, insecure side came out and I opened my big mouth, "So is that what you say to all the girls you kiss?"

He instantly looked hurt, like I'd just slapped him across the face. "No I don't."

I felt like an insensitive jerk. "I'm sorry, I'm just nervous and don't know how I should feel or what I should say to you. Jacob, our spontaneous kissing after seeing each other after all these years. You just don't know, but that is totally not me. I'm a cautious woman. I think before I do something impulsive. And now, I just meet you again and I have my tongue in your mouth, my legs around your waist and enjoyed your hands on my rear end. I'm clearly not myself today. I don't think we should see each other again because I am out of control when I'm with you."

"Well I don't know about your thought processes, but I'm really enjoying the carefree you that's been with me today. You know I think a goodbye kiss would help you clear this crazy talk you are giving me right now. You don't have to be afraid with me, you've known me most of your life."

"I'm not afraid of you, I'm just afraid of how I feel when I'm with you."

He smiled as I leaned in for another chance to be near him. Once again, his strong hand pulled me to him, and in seconds I was somehow in his lap with my rear end sitting on the steering wheel. We were kissing with the passion of two star crossed lovers. My body was like a magnet moving to his every touch. We were connected in a way I couldn't escape even if I wanted to. I could not believe how strongly I felt for him. It was an intensity I'd not felt before and I felt lost and found at the same time. How is this possible?

"Jacob, I've got to go inside to be with my Partner, my family."

"When will I see you again?"

Barely able to catch my breath, I gave in and practically begged him, "Why don't you come by tomorrow sometime?"

"I'll be here, Jenna. For you, I'll be here."

"Okay. Thanks, Jacob, and I'll see you tomorrow."

Chapter 6

Back at the Farm

I went inside, out of breath, flushed, and barely able to find the strength to walk. My brother looked at me and stood at the door while Jacob drove his white Ford pickup out of the driveway.

"Pick-up truck, seems appropriate for Jacob, don't you think?"

"What do you mean by that, Jeffrey? He's a farm boy, so why wouldn't he have a truck to haul things?"

"You know Jacob and his Grandma practically own this entire state. They go and do as they please, and they don't take crap from anyone. You are a novelty to Jacob, fresh meat, something new in the neighborhood. In a week, he'll be charming someone else who walks into his web. He's got a string of broken hearts all over the country. There's a reason he's never married, Jenna. Think about it."

"Why in the world are you saying all this about Jacob? Maybe he's just never met the right girl. And I can assure you, he isn't gay. Don't hold being single against him. At least he isn't divorced with a failure tied to his name."

"No Sis, I'm not saying he's gay; I'm just saying that sometimes people with lots of money think they can buy and sell other people. They don't treat people like they have feelings, they treat people like they are disposable, interchangeable, and replaced at a whim."

"Jeff, that's not fair, you don't even know him as a man."

"Well just how well do you really know him? You just got here, you've been gone what an hour and you're the authority on Jacob the man?"

"Jeff, I love you and value your opinion. I know you just don't want to see me hurt. I appreciate your input but right now let's not talk about my love life. How's Partner doing?"

"You do realize that Partner is not long for this world. It's a matter of hours in all probability. I would be surprised if he makes it till tomorrow this time."

We just stared at each other without saying another word for a few moments. Then Jeff broke the silence. "The last of our cousins are all landing in about an hour and on different flights. Do you want to go with me to pick them up? Troy and Mike are flying in on later flights."

"If there will be room for them, their luggage, and me, then sure I'll go along for the ride. Maybe my luggage will be there by now?"

The rest of the night was sort of a blur. Between trips to and from the airport we sat around Partner's fireplace in the living room looking at pictures, telling stories, playing cards, and discussing trips to Partner's and memories we had all shared as kids. Even with the somber over tones, there was much laughter in the family room. I think it was good for Granny to hear bursts of laughter upstairs as she sat with Partner, reminding her of the joys we share as a family, and that we are here for each other during the hard times.

None of the grandkids made it to our bedrooms that first night. The siblings took the bedrooms, and the grandkids stayed up until I exclaimed, "Is it 5:30 a.m.? No wonder we're all slap happy and exhausted. I'm starving. Let's get our showers and fix breakfast for everyone. Partner always loved a big breakfast every morning."

I jumped into the shower and felt like a new person, fresh, clean, and energetic considering no sleep. My luggage had arrived, so I now had clean clothes to wear. I wonder what Jacob's doing right now. I don't even know where he works or when he leaves for work. Was Jeff right; am I just the flavor of the month to him? Am I just exciting because I'm leaving in a few days and he knows that? *Back to reality Jenna, focus on your purpose here, to be here for Partner and family.*

As I headed downstairs to the kitchen to start breakfast for the family, I heard a light knocking on the front door. Who in the world could that be at Granny's house at 6:16 in the morning? It must be a Hospice nurse.

I beat Jeff to the door and there was Jacob standing in the doorway arms full. Two of his brothers, Francis and Andrew, were behind him with their arms full of food, too. They had carafes of coffee, and boxes of food: cooked eggs, fried and scrambled, bacon, sausage, ham, pancakes, danishes and fresh fruit.

I stood in the middle of the doorway blocking any easy way in or out of the house. Jeff smelled the food and pushed me to the side. Apparently, I was not able to talk or move on my own at that particular moment. Jeff and the cousins invited the boys inside with the food. We thanked them for the food and drinks as Granny came out of her room in a green matching gown, robe, and house slippers. She looked so cute. I know she didn't get much sleep, but she obviously wanted to be in the middle of what was going on at that moment.

"Oh, Jacob, you sweet dear man. And Francis and Andrew so good of you to come over. Thank you. You are so kind to come and check on us. Have you heard Grandpa is failing? Do you want to go in and say goodbye? He's not expected to last the day."

Jacob gently hugged Granny, and walked respectfully and quietly up the wooden steps to Partner's room. The brothers said they wanted to remember Partner with the memories they had, and stayed downstairs.

I looked at Jacob as he came down the stairs and both his eyes were red. I almost lost it; there is a knot in my throat. I took Jacob's hand asked him and his brothers if they could join us for breakfast. They said they had to get back to work. Jacob just smiled. I walked him to the door and stepped out on the front porch with him for a moment. I was really glad I had just taken a shower and brushed my teeth before he showed up this early morning.

Jacob led me to the side of the house, scooped me in his arms, and kissed me hard and passionately. Every time I see him, I want him more. This is ridiculous. I'm acting like someone I don't even recognize. I have no power with this man. I really don't have any idea what I'm doing when it comes to Jacob. My brain shuts off and my heart takes over completely. Who is Jacob and why does he make me feel this way? I see this colder distant man with his own Grandma and a loving caring man with my Granny and Partner. What is it about him that I'm so madly attracted to besides his obvious massive good looks? Why do I give Jacob so much of my thoughts, my time, my body, and so completely? I'm not acting cautious; I'm just living in the moment. This is new for me, but is it right?

I whispered in his ear, "When will I see you again?"

"Let me have your phone."

I handed it to him. He entered his name and number.

"I'll be here when you want me to be here."

I blurted out, "I want you here with me now."

"Okay." He walked over to his truck and talked to his brothers. I heard him say, "I'll deal with her; you just tell her what I said."

I rushed over to his truck. "Jacob, I'm sorry I'm being selfish. You have work to do, and I'll be fine. Go ahead and do what you had planned. We can get together when you are off work."

"No, if you want me here with you, I want to be with you however I can spend time with you, and I'll take as much time as I can get."

Was this man in sales? Cause he is such a smooth talker, indicating lots of practice. I kissed him again as his brothers drove away without him. I heard Jacob groan in a quiet, low, intimate lovers' sound that made me want to forget my relatively conservative upbringing, and consider ripping off our clothes and finding a private place we could be up close and personal. I didn't care about anything but him at that moment. But my common sense came back online, and I regained my composure; I took his hand, and lead him back into the house. I needed my family as my safety net, so I didn't do something I'd regret. Jacob made me want to do and think about things I hadn't done or thought about longer than I care to admit.

Everyone is getting up and around, the smells of delicious food a tasty motivator. Granny takes Jacob's hand as we walked back into the house. "Thank you for bringing all the food and for coming to see Partner." She offered to pay him for the food.

He shook his head, hugged her, and said, "That's what neighbors do, we take care of one another."

She smiled and hugged him back, then noticed we are holding hands. She let go of his hand, stood back for a moment and stared at us. We just kept holding hands. She has a questioning look on her face, but with so many in the kitchen, she didn't start with the hundred questions, thank the Lord! I know that in my near future, Granny will be sending me a long letter, and Jacob will be the main topic of her discussion. Granny didn't do email or internet stuff, because she is old school. She was old-fashioned before old-fashioned became old.

Granny loves to write letters. Writing letters is her way of preaching and teaching her family lessons of life that she thinks we need to know or be reminded of. She has a way of telling you what you are doing is wrong and that she doesn't approve. Granny is famous with all the cousins for her letters. It got to be a joke among us in later life. My cousin Mike got a tattoo and we all said in unison, when Granny sees your ink, you'll be getting a letter! It is kind of fun now as an adult to get them. We are more mature, can laugh about them, and not take them so personally and seriously like we did as children. Not so much fun to get them as a teenager when she's telling me I shouldn't be "swapping slobbers" (what she called kissing) with anyone until I got married. And she'd always send a little brochure about God and how to live a good Christian life in her letters. I always wondered what kind of life does she think I live, to send me mini sermons every month?

With her one-way communication, she always means well and loves me but after years of letters, I learned it is best to be sitting alone with a glass of wine and chocolate to recover from the letter as quickly as possible. I love my Granny and her wanting me to be better than I am. I just didn't appreciate her letters on such a frequent basis and so judgmental. I'm sure one day when she's gone, I will miss someone caring about me that much, and in her way.

After breakfast, Granny asked each of us to write down stories about special times we shared with Partner. She wanted us to find pictures of everyone in the family with Partner to make a slide show for the funeral. He's not even dead yet and we are planning his funeral. It didn't seem quite right, but it gave us something useful to do with our time and energy.

Wonderful. Jacob is going to see pictures of me through all the awkward years... birth up till now. He probably won't mind the now so much but when he is reminded of my younger photos, oh brother it will just jog his memory of what a dork I was as a kid.

Jeff came into the living room and sat right next to Jacob. What are brothers for right? My darling cousins were all present and eating around the large wooden dining room table. They started asking Jacob all sorts of prying questions.

It is like they are interviewing him for me. I am embarrassed and don't know if I should laugh or cry. But I wanted to know answers to these questions too, so I just smiled, held his hand, and listened. Jeff asked what he did for a living and even how much money he made a year. I wanted to kick him under the table for being inappropriate, but I knew if I did, he'd just say out loud, "Jenna, why did you kick me under the table?" And all the cousins would crack up. So, I just had to sit here like a bump on a log. They didn't give Jacob a break, not for a minute. The morning flew by. By the time everyone got around, showers, breakfast, airport shuttles, it was almost time for lunch. How could I be hungry again?

"Jacob, are you interested in taking me to town to pick up supplies for Granny?" I'm thinking about all the extra company Granny will be having in the house. She will need plenty of toilet paper, milk, bread, eggs, and the general basics. I want to make sure she has what she needs and doesn't have to worry about needing something.

"Sure, I'll volunteer to go with you, anything to get out of the hot seat of interrogation from your brother and cousins. Is now too soon?"

My cousins are all smiles, probably impressed with their detective work. After telling my mom where we are going and what we are doing, I gave her, my aunt, and Granny hugs then quickly walked out the front door with

Jacob. I turned around and shook my pointer finger at the interview team. With that, they all busted out into roaring laughter. Glad I could lighten their moods. A little distraction isn't too bad considering what we are facing with Partner even if it is at Jacob's expense.

It's going to be a long day, but I'm so happy that Jacob is here by my side in this difficult time. If he is nothing but eye candy, he'd be worth the distraction today! But my mind is racing with so many things; will Jacob treat me differently in town where he knows everyone? When people see us together in public what will he say or do? It will be interesting to watch how he treats me and I'm trying to guard my heart by watching what's happening around me. I don't want to get hurt, or to hurt Jacob. *At least I'm thinking logically again. This is me, I'm back, mind over heart, thinking over feeling. Be logical Jenna and welcome back to reality.*

Jacob said he needed to get his truck and that he'd be back to take me to town. He was back in less than thirty minutes.

I had asked him to see if Ms. Ruth needed anything while we headed to town. Living in a farming community, trips to town are thirty to forty highway miles one way, so you try to make each trip count.

In the daylight it's especially beautiful here. The rolling hills, deep green grass, horses in the fields, miles and miles of dark brown fencing alternated with miles and miles of white fencing. It is all so stunning and relaxing, like coming home. The warmth of the sun beating in on the windows of the truck, great music on the radio, the lack of sleep the night before, and the stress of Partner's final hours hit me and at some point I fell asleep on our way to town. I heard a deep, gentle voice say my name, "Jenna, Jenna, wake up, we're here."

Chapter 7

The News

I opened my eyes and my head was on Jacob's shoulder and his arm was around me. He was unfastening my seatbelt. My legs were curled up in the seat and he was smiling down at me. Are you kidding? I fell asleep. How is this possible, with an incredible hunk of a man by my side. Ludicrous. This could only happen to me.

I sat up and quickly checked myself in the rearview mirror. Not as bad as I had imagined I looked, not wonderful, but under the circumstances... whatever.

"Jacob, I'm so sorry I wasn't good company for you. How long did I sleep?"

"Only about an hour."

"An hour, I thought it is only a forty-minute drive."

"It is, but I pulled over and let you rest for a while. Jeff told me you guys didn't sleep last night and I didn't want you getting sick with the stress of your Grandpa's condition."

If I wasn't worried about having morning breath after my nap, I would kiss him then and there. I just smiled. "Thank you. You are very thoughtful."

"Jenna, let's eat lunch first then we can get the groceries and head back to your Granny's. This is the best place in the area for lunch."

I was dying for a Diet Dr. Pepper, so I was all in for caffeine and munchies. Here we are in his territory and he's not treating me any different than he did when I was with him privately. That's a good sign. The waitress came over to our booth all smiles for Jacob and a scowl for me.

"Alice, this is Mr. Bilmont's Granddaughter, Jenna."

Only after hearing who I am related to, did she give me a sweet smile. She put her hand on my shoulder. "We all love your Grandpa. He is the sweetest man ever; well next to Jacob that is... so sorry to hear his health is failing. He will be missed."

"Thank you."

She went to get our drinks and I wondered how could she know about Partner?
Jacob must have read my questioning expression. "Small towns. People know what's happening before it happens."

"Jacob, I'm really sorry about my brother and cousins asking you all those questions. I had nothing to do with that. I am glad to find out things about you, but if I want to know something, I just ask. They are just protective of me. You handled their questions with humor and class. Thanks for being a good sport."

"I will tell you anything you want to know. However, since you found out every possible detail about me through the interrogation process this morning, how about I ask some questions about you now? Turnabout is fair play don't you think?"

"Okay, that seems fair. What do you want to know?"

"Hmmm, what's the most important thing to you in a relationship?"

Wow what a thoughtful thing to ask. His first thought is about me and my feelings and what it would take to have a successful relationship? Very unexpected and very impressive. He couldn't have asked me a better first question if he had planned it.

"That's easy Jacob, for me without a doubt it's honesty. If you don't trust someone, you can't count on him, you don't have a relationship. You can tell the truth a million times, but it only takes one lie, to make a person doubt everything you say after that. Please don't ever, ever lie to me. I'd rather be hurt with the truth once, than over and over with a lie. A liar is a deal breaker for me."

"So, do you have trust issues?"

"If you're connected to people in this life, you will probably have some kind of trust issues. I guess it would be fair to say I don't trust easily. I think you should know that back home I am in love . . . "I pause to see if he makes any facial expression. "With my dogs, Molly and Moose. Jacob had a relieved smile on his face. He didn't ask another question, so I continued. "You already know I am a kindergarten teacher. I love teaching, love the kids, but not wild about where I'm living."

"Do you mean your home, the city, or state?"

"I mean I love my house because it's mine, my personality, peaceful and full of love with family, friends, and Molly and Moose. But I'm not wild about the state I'm in. It's high humidity in the summer and icy in the winter. I like having four seasons. The trees are so beautiful in the fall. People are nice there, but there are other places I would rather live. Have you ever been married before? Engaged? I think I went to the bathroom when my family asked you those questions. I didn't hear what you said."

"I guess my turn to ask you questions is over? No to being married before and yes to being engaged."

"What happened?"

"Long story short, she was a model and had modeling

engagements that weekend. We had an argument, one of many, and I broke up with her for the last time over the phone. She said she was headed to my place after her jobs to change my mind. I did care about her, but she wanted a different lifestyle than I did, and we weren't meant to be together. After her modeling assignment, she was on her way to my house when a drunk driver went over the center line. The accident killed her instantly. It nearly killed me too.

"I'm so sorry, Jacob. How long ago?"

"It's been three years now. How about you? I assume, by the way you kissed me, you aren't married. So are you engaged, divorced, both, neither?"

"No and yes and what do you mean you assume the way I kissed you I'm not married?"

"Which answer is yes, and which one is no?"

Before she could answer the waitress arrived with their food. "Who had the grilled chicken sandwich, cottage cheese and lettuce salad with blue cheese dressing?"

"That's Jenna's. I had the steak sandwich, salad with Ranch, and fries."

"It looked like you were in deep conversation, I hated to interrupt." She wiped her hands on the front of her apron. "Can I get anything else for you?"

"I'll take another Diet Dr. Pepper if you don't mind, thanks."

"That will be all for me, thanks Alice."

"Alice, first name basis, hum. Ever date pretty Miss. Alice?"

"Once or twice we've gone out."

"I see."

"Really, what do you see?"

"My observation is that you are single, handsome, okay very handsome, and successful; of course you are going to date a lot. In a small farming community, any woman that's nice looking has probably dated you at some time or other.

That's what I'm thinking."

Jacob smiled. "You should eat your food before it gets cold. We can discuss your engagements and or divorce on our way to the grocery store and on the way home."

"Okay and by the way, you were right, this food is delicious. The chicken is so tender and juicy I can cut it with my fork."

"I wouldn't lead you astray, Ms. Jenna, or is it Mrs. Jenna?"

"That will be a conversation on our drive home, more private and less staring eyes."

Jacob looked around the restaurant and everyone diverted their gaze.

"Are you some kind of celebrity in this area? What is it with people and staring? First it is your brothers staring at me at your Grandma's place, now at your community eatery. Seriously what's the deal?"

"Maybe they aren't used to seeing me with such a beautiful woman."

"Thank you but I'm being serious."

"So am I."

"Do you have the grocery list?"

"Yep it's right here, and nice way to change the subject. Are you ready to go?"

"Yes, let's go."

"I need to use the restroom first and I'll meet you at the truck." I went back to the restroom and Jacob kindly paid our bill. As I am sneaking a sip of water out of the faucet in the bathroom, to rinse away any food particles so I can kiss Jacob if the opportunity presents itself later. Alice walked into the bathroom, shut the door behind her, and stood in the doorway with both of her hands on her hips and a glare for me.

"Hello again. I just wanted to tell you that Jacob is a great guy and we all love him. If you hurt him, he has a long line of girls waiting to comfort him, a long, long line. I just wanted you to know because it looks like you two are a couple, or you want to be a couple, so just know he can see a gold digger a mile away. He won't be lonely, never has been, never will be. I just thought you should know how things are around here."

"Oh…okay, thanks." With that I walked, well I actually had to push my way around Alice to get out of the bathroom, then I walked quickly out to the truck.

"Everything okay?"

"Sure, and thanks for lunch".

Jacob didn't seem convinced but didn't push it. Just as we arrived at the local grocer, my cell buzzed. "It's Jeff, I need to take this."

"Jenna, are you where you can talk?"

"Yes, how's Partner?"

Jeff spoke quieter than usual. "Partner's just taken his last breath, and went to be with Jesus." Then there is silence on the phone.

I had started to get some air by getting out of Jacob's truck, but I couldn't move once I stood up. I just leaned against the truck and started to cry. "Jeff, I love you. We'll be there as soon as we get the groceries."

Jacob got out of the truck, walked around to my side, took me in his arms, and just held me. We stood in the main street of town crying in each other's arms. No talking, just being there for each other. Then he gently kissed me on my eyes, nose, then the lips and I kissed him back. I wasn't thinking at all and didn't realize that we were making out downtown in front of everyone until one man whistled. I looked up to see the store front windows full of people staring again. I looked at Jacob and he sat me back on the seat of his truck.

"I recommend that you stay put in the truck and re-group while I run in and grab the groceries. We'll be on our way back to Partner's in 15 or 20 minutes."

I handed him the grocery list and put my head down on

the seat. I just closed my eyes and rested. I didn't want to see anyone else staring at me anymore. I'm not one of those women who can cry and look beautiful doing it. My eyes swell and my nose runs, it's not pretty on any level. I try to avoid tears if at all possible anytime I feel them coming around. I refuse to watch sad movies because life is too short to waste it being sad and depressed. I've always heard big girls don't cry, it's a sign of weakness, and you don't show your weakness especially in public.

Jacob opened the door to his truck I had fallen asleep yet again.

"I'm sorry for disturbing you, go back to sleep."

But I don't want to sleep, I want to be next to you. I scooted next to him, and he told me to scoot back over and put on my seatbelt. He kind of hurt my feelings but I did as he directed. He said he lost one woman he loved in an accident; he would make sure I was safe when I was on the road. I hadn't thought of that from his perspective and am glad he explained what he is thinking and why he's acting the way he did. He isn't rejecting me, he's protecting me. It made me like and adore him more if that is possible. He didn't bring up the question about me being engaged or divorced and I didn't want to talk about anything that took any energy. I felt sad and drained.

"What can I do to help you?"

"Thank you for being with me today. You have made a terrible day bearable. I'm usually a pretty cautious person, but I have strong feelings for you, and this is really surprising to me. This is so sudden, it is sort of shocking."

Jacob smiled and said, "Right back at cha babe." His turn of phrase didn't set well with me. It sounded rehearsed, like he'd said it many times before and to many different women before me.

It sort of ticked me off. I was being honest and he responded with an off the cuff comment. So, I just turned away from him and looked out my window in silence. I'm tired, stressed, and don't want to deal with a possible relationship right now anyway.

"What... did I say something wrong? Jenna, don't give me the silent treatment. Hey look at me. Don't shut me out. Tell me what you're thinking."

Great, a man who can read my poker face. I pride myself in being honest, so here goes. I told him how I felt, how I am vulnerable right now. I told him how I feel about him and how it hurt that he threw out some phrase he's used a hundred times before on every other woman he's been with, when I needed something personal and heartfelt.

"Jenna, I'm sorry I didn't think of all that when I said it, but I didn't say it to be unkind or hurtful. I have very strong feelings for you too, and I'm not sure what to do or where to go from here." Then he smiled and said, "I know where I'd like to go, what I'd like to do with you, but I don't think under the circumstances it's appropriate."

I gave him a semi-grin and *thought sure... he wants to have sex with me, but not a relationship. He just sees me as some fresh meat in the area. Just like Jeff warned me. Get yourself together Jenna and focus on your family and Partner. Jacob isn't your priority, focus on my family. Just enjoy the ride but know he's not for keeps, this is temporary.*

"Jacob, in case I haven't told you earlier, thank you again so much for all you've done for me and my family during our loss. It's been great getting to know you better and seeing Ms. Ruth again."

"Wait a minute, what's happening here? Are you giving me a kind brush off, are you saying goodbye to me right now? Is that what you're doing? When someone gets too close to you emotionally, you push him away? Is that how you are? Is that why you're single?"

"Jacob, what do you want from me? Honestly, sex or a relationship? I don't know what you want. I can't read your mind. You said if I want to know something just ask, so tell me."

"Jenna, can't we have a sex filled relationship?"

"Knock off the humor, Jacob, I'm serious. I don't know what to think, or what to do. What do you want? Be honest with me because I don't do games. I feel pressured with my Partner's passing and my family needing me, so I feel like we are on a time crunch here."

"Jenna, don't you know by now, I want you. I've loved you since you were a little girl and you tried to sit cross legged on top of my palomino Goldie. What normal red-blooded American does that? Then my horse kicked at a fly, you lost your balance and fell off Goldie into that huge pile of manure. You stood there, manure all down your left side, and wouldn't say a word, not a tear, no excuse, nothing. You just took the reins of that horse and lead her all the way back to the barn amid our laughter.

"Right then and there, I knew you were special, and I was smitten, always have been. I don't know why I never asked you out before. I guess you were more like a kid sister I never had back then. I can say that's not the case now."

"I don't even know if you're engaged, divorced, or both. Part of me doesn't even care. Ever since our first kiss when you didn't just do a polite lip service, you gave me all you had, I couldn't get enough. I've never been with a woman who was willing to trust me and give me all of her like you did at our first embrace."

"Jenna, you touched me to my inner core. I told you that if you'll recall. I really care about you and want you in my life. You are smart, funny, caring, and sexy as hell. I keep thinking about you getting on a plane in a few days and leaving me. I am lost in thoughts of what to do to make you stay. I've become a desperate man since we kissed. You make me anxious and excited. I need you in a way I've never known before now. I want to know you more. I'm a guy and not used to talking all this emotional girl talk, but this is what I've figured out about how I feel about you so far."

"Pull over, Jacob."

Chapter 8

The Officer

"What?"

"Pull over, I'm taking off this seat belt, so you can pull over or not, but I strongly suggest you pull over, because the seatbelt is coming off in 5-4-3-2-1."

Jacob threw his arm across my chest to hold me back and he pulled the truck to a screeching stop at the side of the road. I was out of my seatbelt and in his arms before the truck had stopped its quick stop motions of an emergency stop. We were locked into each other's embrace. My mind racing, how could such a great guy fall for me? He barely knows me, and I barely know him, but I think I love him. I want him like I always dreamed I could want someone. It was like a movie and I am the leading lady, and I am the most beautiful, desired woman in the world, with the most handsome man in the world. Jacob wants me, he said so. If this doesn't last, will I regret if I don't show him how I feel? I'm not holding back with him. I want him, he wants me.

Partner's gone now, and there is family to help Granny and mom at the house, so for now, it's just Jacob and me. I don't want to think, I just want to feel the love of this gorgeous man.

Jacob and I were in the truck lost in our emotions and desires when Jacob whispers in his heavy breathing breaths, "You deserve better than a pickup truck by the side of the road for our first time Jenna."

I looked in his eyes, and at that moment noticed flashing lights. Jacob must have seen them at the same time, because he pulled himself off of me and we sat up just as the police officer knocked on the truck window on the driver's side. Jacob rolled down the window.

"Hello Jacob, I thought this was your truck. Is everything okay? I see skid marks on the road where you pulled off the road in a hurry. I can smell the burnt tire smell. Is everything okay?"

Jacob just sat staring at this man. I couldn't tell if he knew him and he was just joking around with him, or if he didn't like him and he wasn't going to say anything. Finally, I broke the long awkward silence.

I leaned over Jacob and spoke "I'm sorry officer, I wasn't feeling well, and so he pulled over quickly. Then I felt faint (*after our kissing that part was true*), and he had me lie down. My grandfather just died and he's taking me there now."

"I'm sorry for your loss ma'am. Who's your grandfather?"

Jacob finally spoke in a firm authoritative tone. "Donny, its Mr. Bilmont, he just passed away. Now if you don't mind, I need to get her and their groceries to Mrs. Bilmont's place."

The officer gave Jacob a sort of sad look then told us to drive safely and we were snapped into the seatbelts and were on our way back to the farm.

"You know officer Donny, don't you?"

"Yes."

"You didn't seem to be on good terms with him."

"Jenna, you don't need all this baggage right now."

"I'm stronger than I look, tell me, honesty remember. I just want to know everything about you, and I could use the distraction…."

"Okay, you asked for it, but I really don't think this is the time for this conversation."

"Jacob, if you don't want to talk about it, I'll respect your wishes. I don't know where this conversation is going, and if you don't want to share, I'll respect your privacy. Don't feel pressured, I just felt tension between you two and didn't understand it that's all."

"No, I'll tell you about the tension. Donny was on duty, chasing a drunk driver, and that drunk driver lost control and killed my fiancé. That's all I know about Donny since the accident."

"You were good friends with Donny before the wreck, but haven't spoken since then? It's been three years and you've not spoken to him in this small town? He was only doing his job, right? He was just trying to get a drunk driver off the roads so he wouldn't kill someone. It's the drunk driver you should be mad at, not him, Jacob. He was just doing his job. Am I right or am I missing something here?"

"The drunk driver was Donny's wife. They had a fight that night and she took off in her car and he was chasing her in his police car, then the accident." Silence……

"Oh, I'm so sorry, I don't want to cause you pain, not now, not ever. I just want to know everything about you. Thank you for putting those pieces together for me. I hope you can forgive him someday, for your sake."

"Let's talk about another subject. I'm here for you. I'm fine. I'll walk you into your grandparent's house with groceries then I'll leave if you want it to just be your family. But if you'll let me, I want to be by your side. You just let me know and I'll do whatever you want."

"Don't say anything unless you mean anything."

"I said it, I'll stand by it within reason because I'm a reasonable person. If we are both reasonable why, what's that look?"

"Jacob would you be game if I wanted to sneak you upstairs to the bedroom I'm staying in and have wild passionate sex with you? Would you be up for that tonight?"

"Did you hear the "reasonable adult part? No way Jenna! I would not be up for that. The way your brother and your cousins watch after you, we wouldn't get to first base before they would have me hanging from a rope. But thanks for giving me that visual picture of us. I'll hold on to it until I can get the real thing."

"Jacob, seriously I don't know if I'll be worth the wait."

"Oh, I know you will be. Speaking of being ready, are you ready?"

"Ready for what?"

"We're at your Grandma's house. Are you ready to go inside?"

"Oh…"

How conflicted can one person be? Part of me is so sad for my Granny, she was married 70 years and now Partner's gone. What will Granny do now? And the other part of me is so happy and alive for the first time in many years. I've reconnected with Jacob and he's turning out to be the man of my dreams. So unexpected, I'm so happy. All I can think of is him and how I want him in my life, in my bed, in my heart and home. When I'm with him I feel like I'm at home with my best friend who happens to be the sexiest man alive. He's my comfy jeans. I feel comfortable to tell him anything. My friends back home would never believe this or that I'm acting this way! I'm not even sure I believe this is true myself.

As we walked into Granny's house with the groceries, Jeff met us at the door. "Thanks for taking Jenna around town and running errands. I'm sure you need to get back to your job and your family. We're here for each other, we're good if you need to go. We will take care of Jenna."

"Jeff, I'm here for Jenna too, and I'm staying until she asks me to leave."

"Well I'm her brother, and I'm asking you to give her some breathing room. She just lost her Grandpa and she doesn't need an opportunist taking advantage of her trusting good nature when she's vulnerable and hurting."

"I'm not taking advantage of anyone, especially Jenna. I care about your sister and want to be here for her. I know she adores you, and if you want me to go, she would ask me to go for your benefit. If you love her as much as she loves you, you'd trust your sister and let her live her own life and let her make her own decisions."

"That's rich coming from a man who lives off his Grandma's power and money."

"You don't know anything about my business! I know you are upset because you lost your grandpa today, so I'll let that one slide."

I came rushing back to the door after putting my groceries in the kitchen. "That's enough guys, what's going on in here?"

"Jenna, Jacob was just headed to his place, he's leaving."

"Jacob, do you need to leave so soon?"

"Only if you want me to go, I'm free to stay as long as you want."

"Gentlemen, I can cut the apprehension in here with a knife. Can we all just get along please?"

Jeff rolled his eyes and walked out of the doorway into the living room. The cousins all standing around looking at me and Jeff, then they followed him into the kitchen where all the family was gathered.

"I know your brother loves you, he's protective of you, and that's what a good guy would do for his little sister, I get it. He sees me as someone taking advantage of you when you are in a vulnerable state. He might be right. I'm not sure that it's not intentional if I am... I'm lost in my feelings for you and just want to spend every waking moment with you, and the sleeping ones too, come to think of it. I think I've fallen for you Jenna. I'm not leaving just because your brother wants me to go. I'll win him over in ten or twenty years from now when he sees how much I love and adore you. We are going to make this work. But I will leave if you want me to leave. I don't want to make things more difficult for you or your family. I just want to be here for you and with you."

"Jacob, you know I have strong feelings for you too, it may even be love, but my family is hurting right now, and I don't want to do or say anything that would cause them extra stress or worry. I need to put their needs before my personal happiness right now. Maybe you should go, but just for now."

"If that's what you want, I'm gone."

"Not forever Jacob, just for now. Can I call you later?"

"Whatever you want, I'll do whatever you ask."

"Are you mad?"

"Yes."

"Why?"

"You are worried about my Grandma running my life, but you let your brother run yours."

"That's not fair."

"Isn't it?"

"Jacob, you should go. I don't have the energy to argue with you right now. I don't want to hurt you, I'm just trying to do what's right here. But I'll call you later."

"No need to walk me out, I know the way."

Jeff walked back into the living room and quickly

walked over and shut the door behind Jacob. Then he quietly came over to the couch and sat beside me. We just sat there with all the tears and sorrow and pain on loved ones' faces. Even with all the noise of the family in the house, where plans were being compiled for Partner's funeral, and all the commotion going on, I sat there at the table, but I'm numb.

Partner is gone, and so is Jacob. Jacob just told me he loves me and what did I do? I told him I'd call him later and he should leave. What is wrong with me? The house is full of family and love, and loss, and I have never felt lonelier in my life. What had I done? *What should I do? I need to think, logic over emotion Jenna. I need sleep. I always think clearer when I've rested and given myself time to reflect on a situation, instead of reacting in the heat of the situation. I need clarity.*

Chapter 9

The Funeral

I had forgotten how much was involved behind the scenes when someone dies; all the phone calls, emails, Facebook notifications, funeral home visits, church visits, newspaper obituary, all the people coming by the farm, bringing food, and visiting. All the places to contact and communicate with when someone you love has passed away. It is almost overwhelming. I am so glad I have a great family to cover all the different things that need to be done in order to honor my Grandpa.

The boys have been out mowing the yard, weed eating, and checking out the porch to nail down loose boards. Others were checking the oil in Granny's car and air in her tires, etc. With all the people coming to see Granny, they want her place to look its best and she appreciated their expressions of love. What a great team of men I'm related to. I am blessed! I tried to write down names of all the people who came to show their condolences and what they brought to the farm so we can get their dishes back to them. The house is full of flower arrangements making it smell like a florist shop, so fresh, fragrant, and lovely. It reminds me there is beauty in the midst of great sorrow.

Partner had people that knew him all their lives and lots of family and friends wanting to attend his final farewell tribute. He is loved and respected and I am touched. Grandpa still fit into his military uniform, so Grandma wanted him to wear that for his eternal rest. Some of his buddies made arrangements to have a military funeral. Partner played the trumpet, so the military performed a trumpet salute. After folding the flag that is placed over his coffin nice and tight, they presented the triangle to Granny. Lastly, they concluded with a three-gun salute. Partner would have smiled with that farewell of love and respect. He was all U.S.A. Country and God were first in his thoughts and conversations. It is kind of his buddies to make these arrangements for Partner.

When my dad passed away, I was lost in emotional turmoil to the point my brain sort of shut down. So I could cope with the loss, I guess. I could see people, and move, but my thoughts were sort of in a fog. I pushed myself to remember to put one foot in front of the other and to sit and not cry all the tears that were bursting to pour out. I remember seeing faces and my heart would overflow with love, feeling overwhelmed knowing friends and family came to support my brother and me during our loss. It actually still touches my heart thinking about those who went out of their way to be there during our time of need. I see their faces and appreciate each one of them more than they will ever know. It's important to be there for friends and family. Words may not be said between you at the time, but the memories play over and over.

I guess knowing that Partner had lived a full, healthy life but was slipping mentally and physically at the end, somehow made it easier for me to deal with his passing.

Maybe it was because Partner died of natural causes and dad died from cancer made a difference too. I don't know for sure. Saying goodbye to someone you love is never easy and it takes time to process the pain of that loss. It takes an even longer time to deal with the grief after the funeral. Part of me still misses my dad every day and it's going on two years now. I keep waiting for my heart to get over it, but it's always that dull pain inside I just try to navigate around. I still go to call him and remember I can't anymore.

I call my brother and his voice and mannerisms are so much like dad's it sometimes catches my breath. No one can fill the void left in your life when you lose someone you truly love. We are all uniquely created and each has individual gifts and talents. We just have to hold on to the memories of those special loved ones imprinted on our hearts. I will hold Partner's and my Dad's memories forever. It helps to share those memories with stories of things they did and said that were funny, or crazy, or just those special moments shared through the years. Those are the things we remember. I love to take pictures, so I go through photos of my dad when I'm missing him and it helps to see his handsome face. It will remind me of a happy memory and that's part of why I love photography so much.

My mom's family has been raised going to church and living by the golden rule: Do unto others, as you would have them do unto you. My Partner made sure his family was in church anytime the church doors were open. That was basically Sunday mornings and nights, Wednesday nights and an occasional Saturday Night for Christ Ambassadors – the youth group celebrations. He loved to sing, and any family gathering wouldn't be complete unless there was music: guitars, piano (if available), singing, four-part harmony and lots of love. And always a group prayer when we ate a meal together and when we were leaving to go back home. The only exception was during harvest time. Other than that, all were in church when the church doors were open. It was Partner's social time too. He loved to visit.

That is my spiritual heritage. I can still see my Partner standing in front of his church leading the song service waving his arms to the tempo and singing *How Great Thou Art* with his smiling face encouraging everyone to join in and sing from their soul.

I too hold a strong faith in God and believe that I will see Partner again. Today my sorrow is strong and real, I miss him, but my sadness is temporary because I believe I will see him one day when I'm in heaven. And Grandpa and my dad will be healthy and celebrating my arrival too. Getting through this funeral is going to be emotional for me. I'll do fine as long as I don't see tears. If I see tears, I'm going to be waterworks.

Watching the DVD of pictures we assembled together for Partner's service made me think how quickly time flies by. You hear old people say that all the time, but I'm getting to an age now where I'm realizing this is actually true for me too. Every year seems to go faster than the year before. I don't know how that's possible. I know logically there are 365 days each year. It seems like I was just in high school, college, then graduate school. Now I'm at the age where I am supposed to be grown up and act my age, but I really don't want to admit my age much less act it. I just want to be as honest and as kind as I can be, help others along the way, be a good friend, live in the moment, and appreciate the here and now.

Life is so short, I don't want to waste my time on things that don't really matter. I feel like I get easily sidetracked with things that aren't important in the big picture of my life. I don't know why I do that. I get diverted and let people and situations steal my attention, time and energy, and sometimes my happiness. I should guard my heart and put my energy toward people and things that are meaningful to me. So far that's been easier said than done. I think when you lose someone important to you, it makes you stop and seriously think about what is really important to you and be a little more appreciative to the gift of life. It can be taken from us at any time.

As my mind is racing from the images of the past on the DVD, I nonchalantly looked around the church for Jacob, but he wasn't there. I hadn't heard one word from him since I asked him to leave Granny's house. I've lost sleep over that last conversation with him, replayed it over and over in my mind, changing what I wanted to say and what I should have said from "you should leave" to a more loving, caring comment that reflected more accurately how I felt. But what's done is done, as much as I wish I could change the past, it's not possible. Clearly, I blew it with him.

That's another bad habit I have. I think of great things to say and do after the moment is gone. It's rather frustrating but that's me. I waste time and energy reliving things and replay them in my mind, wishing for different outcomes, but to no avail. I know that's a gigantic waste of time, but I always think if I take the time to figure out what I should have said, the next time I won't make the same mistakes. However, that line of reasoning hasn't worked so far for me. But I keep hoping I will learn from my past mistakes, you know the whole older and wiser thing. I'm waiting for that to happen for me.

Here I had the most beautiful man I've ever met, much less knew. And this amazing kind-hearted man honestly admitted he cared about me to my face, even used the word love. And what did I do? I pretty much slapped him in the face. When it's all said and done, he's in his world and I'm going back to my rather dull life in Missouri in a few days. I guess he was too good to be true, at least for me.

I noticed Ms. Ruth is here at the funeral with four of her boys, and several of her grandsons but Jacob is still nowhere to be seen. My heart is sad and heavy missing him, but you can't make someone be something or someone they aren't. I have enough sorrow with a funeral I don't need to look for more by thinking about losing Jacob too.

Now we are back from the grave side service, sitting in the church banquet room eating a late lunch with family and friends, laughter intermittent with tears. I heard a familiar sound of boots walking down the wooden stairs in the entry of the church. I turned and saw Jacob. My heart jumped for joy. Before I could meet him in the entry way, Jeff and four of my cousins were at the entrance talking to him and blocking his entry. My eyes caught Jacob's and he saw me too. Our eyes remained on each other as I tried to get to him as quickly as I could from across the room. I wanted to run to him but didn't want to make a scene. He stood, not moving, not speaking in the doorway watching me. In what seemed like an eternity, I politely pushed my way through the crowd and finally reached Jacob. Jeff stood directly in front of me, blocking me.

"Jenna, stop! I asked Jacob to stay away from you until you contacted him. Did you ask him to come here today?"

My mind went blank for a moment. Jacob wasn't rejecting me the past few days; he is respecting the wishes of my family. I hadn't called him. I hoped he would miss me and call. I can see he is as miserable as I am. I felt terrible for putting him, and us into this situation. I should have called him. I'm an idiot.

"Jenna, did you invite him?"

"Yes of course he's invited! Now let him through, there's tons of food here, and he looks hungry. Gentlemen please let him in, he is Partner and Granny's friend."

They were all glaring at me like I'd just let in the enemy. All I wanted to do was hug and kiss Jacob and tell him how sorry I am for our last conversation and for not calling him. I took Jacob's hand. His reaction was cold and nonresponsive.

"Jacob, are you feeling alright?"

"Fine."

Great, a one-word answer. If he's anything like me, this isn't a good sign. "Okay, Jacob, if you are going to be cold and distant to me, why did you even bother to come here in the first place? I don't need this, especially today."

"Jenna, enlighten me if you will. Why did you just tell a lie to your brother in a church? Miss honesty is everything and a lie is a deal breaker. You didn't call me or invite me, so why the lie, Jenna? Do your rules only work for others but not for you?"

"Well technically speaking, sir, the newspaper invited all friends and family to the funeral and lunch afterwards so, of course you were invited. And, if you'll recall, I said you were invited. I didn't say I called you and invited you personally."

"That's not what they asked you and you know it. You didn't call me, Jenna. Any particular reason why?"

"Why didn't you call me, Jacob, you have a phone too?"

"Are we really going to play this song and dance?"

"I don't know… are we going to fight at my Grandpa's funeral? If you want to be here for my Granny, then go over and sit by her. If you want to be here for me, then be here for me now. I don't want to fight with you. I just don't have the energy."

Jacob firmly held my arm and directed me to a side Sunday school room. He shut the door behind us and put one hand on each of my arms, about a couple fists below my shoulders. With a wild look in his eyes, he lifted me up off the ground until I was looking at him eye to eye. My feet were dangling in the air and I was pinned against the wall.

It all happened so quickly I didn't have time to be afraid, or speak or object.

"What have you done to me, Jenna? I've sat staring at

my phone for two days waiting for one call from you, or even a quick text. Just to hear your voice, to know you were okay, any little crumb you could throw my way, but nothing. I don't do that Jenna. I don't wait for girls to call me, ever. They wait for me to call them. I want to be with you every second of every day and you? Not even a thought to call me? I've wasted two days thinking about nothing but you and worrying about you, wondering what you're doing.

"Jacob, stop. That's not how it was for me. You've got it all wrong. I'm so sorry I hurt you. Truly, I am deeply sorry. That was never my intention."

"I already cost you one full day off work. I didn't want you to use your days off when I was sad and had my family around me to help work this grieving thing out together. I wanted you to have days saved up so you could possibly fly out and see me if you wanted to and I could fly out and see you if things progressed with us, so we could have time to spend together in a more positive atmosphere. I wanted us to spend time together when we could share good times and make happy memories of us. I'm really sorry I didn't call you. I guess I'm sort of old fashioned that way. I really don't call boys."

"It's not that I didn't think about you. I thought about you a lot, I really did. Jacob honestly, look at me. I wanted to call every day too, but I didn't want you to see me as this sad and needy woman. I wanted you to get to know me as the strong and positive woman I think I am. Not torn up and stressed with all the things that needed to happen to make Partner's final farewell something he'd be proud of. I'm so sorry it translated into you believing I wasn't thinking about you or I didn't care about you, because that is not my truth at all. You have to know I care about you very much Jacob."

"Jenna, you said you wanted a relationship. Well that involves good times and the bad. Not just shutting people out when things don't go all roses and puppy dogs. Do you get that? I told you I cared about you. Do you not believe me Jenna? Do you not trust me? Do you think I just throw my love around to every girl that walks into my Grandma's house? No, I don't do that. Do you hear what I'm telling you? I care deeply for you Jenna. Do you believe me?"

"My mind is such a terrible thing to waste."

"What are you talking about?"

"There's an old country western song running through my mind right now, and the words go something like... *Oh shut up and kiss me!*"

Jacob, still holding me, the stunned look on his face dissolving and turning into a smile. He released the strong grip he had on my arms and was giving me a tender embrace. Then he leaned in and kissed me over and over as we became lost in our passionate kisses. After a few minutes, a knock on the Sunday school door brought us back to attention. It was protective brother Jeff.

"Hey, Sis, is everything okay in there?"

"Yes, Jeffrey we're fine. We'll be out in a minute. We're just having a private word, thanks for checking."

Jacob finally let go of me and my feet were back on the ground. My arms hurt but I was glad we had the time to talk privately and clear up the confusion about our lack of communication over the past few days.

"Okay, I'll see you and Jacob out here in a minute."

"Since we only have a minute, tell me when are you going back home?"

"I don't know. My flight has an open date for the return. I could go back tomorrow or today."

Jacob squeezed me tight again, and whispered, "Don't leave me Jenna, not yet. I just got you back."

"Okay, I made one week of lesson plans for my substitute, but at the end of this week I will have to be home and back to work. I don't want my students to suffer because I found the man of my dreams."

"Wait, so I'm the man of your dreams?"

"Yes, yes, Jacob, you are a dreamboat. Now let's go eat. I'm starving and I'm sure our minute is about up. Don't make Jeff and my cousins come in here and get me."

"I'll go with you to eat now, but tonight you are going to be mine, all mine."

"Oh, you think so?"

"Yes, I know so."

"Well I'm hungry, but now I feel nervous."

"Don't be silly. You need to eat because you will need all your strength for what I have planned for us later. I have some strenuous activities planned for you my dear."

"Jacob, with a sexy smile like that, you might as well take me right here in this Sunday school room, because you are irresistible!"

"No, Jenna, no way. We'll have our time and place together tonight. Now, let's find some food and let Jeff and his posse see that you are still alive and doing fine. And what is with the protective detail the men in your family have over you? Are you in some kind of witness protection detail?"

"Ha, ha very funny, it's just that they love me and don't want to see me hurt again. But one thing you should know before we go out around my family... This will be like our first date. And I want to be clear, I don't put out on the first date." I opened the door and walked out to get into the food line.

Jacob walked with me shaking his head no and staring down at the floor. Then like a submissive puppy, he followed me through the line for food. After we ate, he went on home to plan a date night and whatever it might include.

The lunch was over, and Granny was exhausted. We all carpooled out to Granny's house so she would relax and know we were all comfortable and together. We hoped maybe she would take a nap. No chance on that. Granny was on a second wind or adrenaline rush, something, because there was no talking her into a nap. She wanted to be in the center of anything and everything that was going on. I think she was a little in shock from grandpa's funeral. She is sort of in and out of her mind, going fuzzy and then being there with us in the moment.

But that's what happens when you lose someone you've loved for seventy years. I can't imagine what it would be like to love a man that many years. We would be in conversation and Granny would interrupt with a story about her and Partner. It is a story we've heard many times before, but I think it is therapy for Granny. I think it is her way of processing his departure and her loss.

"Jenna, I would like to have a private word with you if I might."

I knew who Jeff wanted to talk about and it started and ended with Jacob. But if it wasn't for Jeff's kindness, I would have never been able to afford to come out to the funeral in the first place, so in a way, Jeff helped Jacob and me get together. Jeff shuddered at the mention of that fact. My brother's not the only one with a sense of humor. Love my brother, but my Jacob is in a sexy category all by himself. He's so hot he could have his own time zone if that were possible and for some crazy reason, he wants me as much as I want him, which is mind-blowing.

"Sis, all I'm going to say is you need to go slow and get to know him. You know what happened last time, and all the pain and misery you went through. I don't want you to ever go through something like that again. I love you and will support you in whatever you do, but one divorce in your lifetime is more than enough don't you think? Just take it slow with him, you're not desperate, you have options."

"Yes, I hear what you are saying, and I love you. I know you want what's best for me, but I'm finally getting my confidence back and am ready to love and be loved again.

Please be happy for me. Give Jacob a chance, he's been nothing but wonderful to me and to our family for that matter. Jeff, I think this man holds my heart. I didn't want to give it away so quickly. I can't believe this is me acting this way, but in all honesty, I truly adore him. And so far, he's handled me and my heart with tender loving care. Please make the time to get to know him. He's a good guy and I think you'd like him too if you just gave him a chance. I really care about him, I think we have a future together."

Jeff was quiet and rubbing his forehead sort of pacing back and forth. "Okay, if that's what you want. There's no time like the present. Let's do a game of flag football, today."

"Jeff, …what are you saying?"

"You want us to spend time together, get to know each other, so invite Jacob and his brothers to join our family in the field between our houses today at 4:30 for some exercise and fresh air. Unless you don't think your lover-boy is up to the challenge?"

"Oh, I'm sure he's up to it, but sweetie, he's in really good shape. Seriously are you sure this is how you boys, I mean men, will bond by playing sports together?"

"Jenna, you set it up, unless you don't think Jacob is up for a little friendly competition."

"Okay I'll call him and see what he says."

Chapter 10

The Game

"Jacob, it's me, and just so you know, I think it is cute how you entered your phone number on my cell under "A Boyfriend Jacob". I see you didn't want me to scroll down to the "J's" to find you in my phone directory, very clever. You are officially the first name in my contacts."

"Of course, I wanted to be the first name you see every time you look at your phone. Sweetheart, it's so good to hear your voice. I'm so glad you called. Is everything okay? How are you and your Grandma doing?"

"As well as can be expected, thanks for asking, but I have something to run past you… sort of a proposition."

"A proposition from you? You've got my full attention babe, I'm listening."

"Alright, well I was talking to Jeff about us and about wanting him to spend time with you to get to know you better and give you a chance. So, Jeff suggested a friendly game of flag football today in the field between Partner's house and your Grandma's house at 4:30ish. Just like we did when we were kids. Do you think you and your brothers would be interested in playing flag football against the Bilmont family, like old times?"

"Jenna, do you honestly think this is going to be a "friendly" game? We are men now, and things get more competitive. Wait, are you planning on playing?"

"Absolutely, why wouldn't I? If my family is on the field, I'm there too. You have a problem with a girl playing football, Jacob?"

"No, it's not that, I am just thinking we'd be on opposite sides and I didn't like the sound of that."

"Well, keep it in perspective, it's just for this game."

"I don't think this is a good idea."

"Think about it this way. If we play this game together today, then we could count it as our first date. Are you thinking about it?"

"Do you have any second date rules I need to know about?"

"No, can't think of anything at the moment."

"Alright, notify your brother that the game is on! See you on the field at 4:30ish."

"Great, Jacob, I'll see you in your tennis shoes, no cowboy boots for football."

"Babe, cowboy boots are how me and my brothers roll around here."

"No boots, only tennis shoes on the field. That's how it's going to roll. We don't want any injuries, Jacob, so no boots."

"As long as this counts as our first date, then we can go out tonight for our second date, I can't wait see you on the field."

"Oh wait, now that I think about it, my second date rule is usually same rule as my first date rule, but for you, I'm open for negotiation."

"Well then I will be negotiating with you later. And to give you fair warning, I can be very persuasive when I want to be. And, Jenna, I want to be."

"That's exactly what I'm afraid of."

"What you do to me."

Jeff told the cousins that with the stressful few days we'd had, it was time for a game of flag football. All the cousins were in. My cousins were all athletic and in good shape, but how often do you get a team of family or friends together to play this sport? Then Jeff told them the Jamison boys were going to play us as the opposing team. They all immediately stopped and stared at me in questioning silence.

"Guys, this is going to be a fun and friendly game. There are more of us than them, so some of us might have to be on their team. This will be a fun game, fun times, not a mean-spirited game. Right? I'm dating Jacob, so give him and his family a chance. You all grew up with them each summer too. You've hunted and fished together and some of you have gone on trips together. Don't make this into something it's not. We're old friends making new memories in a fun game of flag football. We are representing Partner today boys, and we will conduct ourselves kindly to his neighbors. All in favor say 'I'. Those opposed, don't play."

I didn't give them a chance to respond. "Good, the 'I's have it. The game is at 4:30. Be hydrated and on the field ready to stretch out at 3:45. Any questions ask Jeffrey. This was his idea."

"It's almost 2:30 now, so rest up, we're going to need our strength. I've seen those boys in their short-sleeved shirts, and seriously they are all buff. Those farm boys are going to be a tough crew to beat today men. I mean no disrespect to you cousins, cause you all are fit too, but I'm just saying this is going to be a competition. Do we have a football we could practice throwing and catching before we head to the field?"

Granny came into the room just as I stopped talking. "Hi Granny, how are you doing?"

"I'm fine, darling. What are you kids up to?" I love the fact that no matter how old you are, you're always a kid to your grandma.

"We are going to play a game of flag football in a couple hours. You want to come and watch us play?"

"Where are you kids playing?"

"We thought we'd play in the flat area of field between your house and Ms. Ruth's property. That's a perfect spot to play the game, don't you think?"

"Did you ask Mrs. Jamison if she's okay with us playing there? She is very particular about her things. She probably won't want us on her land so don't get your hopes up."

"No, Granny, it's okay. Her grandsons are going to play with us."

"Oh, honey, I don't think that's a good idea for you kids."

"Granny, I see your hesitation. If you don't want us to play, especially today, we can cancel the game. But, I would really like to know why you don't want us to play with the Jamison's. We grew up playing with these boys and they are your neighbors so if you know a reason why we shouldn't be together, please tell me."

"No, no reason sweet, Jenna, I just don't want anyone to get hurt."

Somehow, I didn't feel she's being honest with us about her reason, but since she just buried her husband of 70 years today, I thought I could cut her some slack and not push her with more questions.

"Granny, we don't want to add any stress to you, especially today. We just thought it would be fun to play and I think if Partner was here and feeling good, he would be playing flag football and throwing horseshoes with us."

"That's fine. Just be sure and pack the lawn chairs

because we are all going to watch this game. I think I will lay down for a quick nap, so I will feel like going with you kids. Be sure and wake me up in case I fall asleep so I can go with you."

"Sure, Granny, we will. You've got time for a good nap, so just rest, we'll take care of everything."

Bathroom breaks done, ice trays emptied into the big, round, five-gallon, yellow water jug and lawn chairs loaded. Bug spray, a lawn blanket, and one referee's whistle. We are ready to rumble. This is actually a fun distraction on such a beautiful Kentucky afternoon.

As all the trucks pulled up in the field, I saw him. His brothers, his Grandma, their relations and hired help in their trucks too. Jacob jumped out all smiles, came up, kissed me on the forehead like I was a little girl, and whispered, "This counts as our first date. This counts as our first date!" I thought he was going to put it to music, dance, and publish a song. "Hope it's good for you, baby."

I didn't have words for his giddy demeanor. I just laughed out loud.

"Jacob, this is going to be fun and safe right?"

"Jenna, you just buried your Grandpa a few hours ago, we are not going to shame your family on the same day."

"Wait a minute, we don't want you to let us win out of sympathy. We want an honest, fair, and fun game. Understand, Mr. Jamison?"

"Sure."

"No, I mean it, Jacob. You tell your brothers they need to play to win."

"Well if you say so, babe."

"Oh, I say so, babe!"

"I think my Jenna might be a little competitive."

"Well she could be, Jacob. So play and you'll soon find out. First, I want to go say hello to your Grandma before we embarrass you out on the field. Then we can start the game."

Jacob's family all had gray, sleeveless tee-shirts on. My family had white tee-shirts on. Several of our shirts were old tee-shirts from Partner's drawer. It was like he was out there with us. Partner had volunteered as a coach for local flag football teams for years and still had the belts with the Velcro flags. We had the red vinyl strips on the sides of each belt and Jacob's team had yellow vinyl flags on each side of their belts. I didn't remember the belts being so small and dingy dirty, but we all got them on so the game could begin.

Jacob's family had marked the field with chalk from their farm supplies so we could see clearly the inbound lines and field goal areas for both teams. It looked like a professional football field. The grass was a little high, and Jacob apologized for not having time before the game to mow the grass.

How sweet of him to do the prep work for our first family time together. A man that wants to please me and works to make it happen, this could be love! I leaned over to give him a good luck kiss. Both teams blew the whistle on us for taking too long on our kiss. We smiled and went to our respective opposite teams. Totally worth the delay of game!

All the sideline observers were in their lawn chairs and ready for the competition. The game was really fun at first. Both teams were being careful, joking around, laughing, and verbally teasing one another. I looked over at the sidelines and both Granny and Ms. Ruth were laughing and enjoying our game on opposite sides of the field. But as the game progressed, competitive attitudes overrode good judgment and the field got progressively rougher. Then it happened... "Boys, if things don't calm down on this field, we will call the game on account of un-sportsman like attitudes. I need everybody to just chill out."

The Jamison's said they'd play fair if we did. The next play, we had the ball and Shawn threw the ball to Troy. It bounced off the tips of Troy's fingers and I caught it before it hit the ground. The fact that I caught the ball was a shock and a miracle wrapped up in one. I held tight and took off running. My first time to actually get the football and I doubted I'd get a second chance for another play. Then I heard Jacob yelling at his brother behind me.

"Don't you touch her!"

After hearing his tone, I was motivated even more. I ran even faster, and that's when it happened. His brother, Andrew full force tackled me to the ground instead of just grabbing one of my flags from my belt. I hit the ground hard with Andrew on top of me and I twisted my ankle. I was in a lot of pain, and thought maybe I had broken it. My brother, Dr. Jeff was right there and said it was probably just a bad sprain. I was doing everything I could not to cry in front of everyone or act like a fragile girl.

"I'd feel better if we went to the hospital and get an x-ray to tell for sure the condition of your ankle. It could be broken. I won't know for sure without an x-ray."

I didn't want to act like it was bad because with my protective family and Jacob's fury with his brother, I just wanted everyone to calm down and keep things in perspective. I didn't want my Granny to worry.

"Jeff, thanks for the offer, but it's really not that bad. It looks worse than it really is. There's no need to worry."

"Andrew, I can't believe you tackled Jenna in flag football. What were you thinking? She's a girl and you flew through the air and slammed her to the ground. Very macho, Andrew! Way to represent the family. She's hurt because of you!"

"Jacob, I said I'm sorry, I don't know what else to do. It was an accident. I feel terrible I'm sorry guys."

I felt sorry for Andrew, and I was the one in pain. But the game was over. I was tired, but with my tackle injury we were the official unofficial winners. Jacob and Jeff helped me hop back to the truck. My foot was now resting in the bottom of our five-gallon water jug of ice-cold water to reduce the swelling and I didn't care how stupid I looked. My foot and ankle hurt so bad I only had one thought, relieve my pain. I thought I was doing a good job acting like it was no big deal, but I didn't think I could keep this brave face for long.

The cousins helped Granny get her chairs gathered up, and they headed back to the trucks. I could hear Granny complaining to my mom.

"I told Jenna this was a bad idea, but she wouldn't listen."

Jacob put his arm around me and asked if we were still on for tonight.

I didn't even get my mouth open to answer before Jeff answered for me.

"No! She's not going out with you or anyone tonight. She will be at the house with her foot up."

I could just imagine Jacob thinking he had plans for my feet to be up in the air tonight too, but I couldn't even make eye contact with him at that moment. I didn't want to see his disappointment. But I pushed through my pain and distress and motioned my finger for Jacob to lean in closer.

"Jacob, I'm so sorry for messing up your plans for us tonight. Please be sure and let Andrew know there are no hard feelings, I know it was an honest mistake. I'll be fine, Jacob, really. I just need to keep the swelling down so I can go back to work when I get home. How about a raincheck on our date?"

"When can I see you?"

"Tomorrow. I'm sure I'll be good as new tomorrow."

Jacob was running his hand up and down on my leg. I had my sweatpants rolled up to above my knee and my foot was back in the five-gallon jug of freezing water. He just stood there again shaking his head in the no motion and apologizing for his brother hurting me.

"Jacob, kiss me so I can go home and have pleasant

dreams about you and me and our date tomorrow."

"Jenna, I'm so sorry you're in pain. I should have never let you play. It was too dangerous. I…"

"Jacob, stop right now! Please do not blow this out of proportion. I wanted to play the game and I was the klutz that twisted my ankle. No one controls me Jacob, not now, not ever. I make my own choices. I'm thankful for the men in my life who are there to help protect me, even from myself sometimes, but I'm fine and capable most of the time. This isn't on you Jacob, it's all klutzy me. Kiss me and I'll see you tomorrow sweetheart."

Jacob still shaking his head said, "Well it's not boring with you, is it, Jenna?"

"You know, I don't get that, because I really am pretty boring. Things just seem to find me that make me seem more interesting than I actually am.",

"I believe you, honey."

"I like it when you call me adoring names. It's so sweet. Get it, you called me "honey" and it's sweet." She did her best to smile through the pain. "Jacob, I can't wait for our real first second date. Kisses until tomorrow my Jacob, see you then."

"Tomorrow can't come soon enough my, Jenna."

"Hum, I like it when you say my name too. Maybe it's just your voice, but I think it's just you. I'll see you tomorrow."

We got back to the house and I didn't have to pretend it didn't hurt so bad. I asked Jeff to help me into bed. He again encouraged me to go to the hospital for x-rays and again I said "No, I just need to clean up and go to bed early, I'll be fine."

So, my Mom and Aunt Elaine helped me so I could get into the bathtub. It was easier to sit with my foot propped up on the side of the tub than to stand on one leg in a wet shower. After I took a cool relaxing bubble bath, I dried off and then went straight to bed. Jeff came by my room and gave me a couple of pills to keep down the swelling. I trusted that bucket-headed brother of mine. But come to find out, he gave me a pain killer and I was immediately out like a light bulb.

Chapter 11

Embarrassments

They came over first thing in the morning to check on me. Jeff greeted him at the door and invited him inside.

"Jacob, Jenna was in a lot of pain last night. She just didn't want anyone to know it. I gave her a pain pill to help her sleep. When she wakes up and realizes that fact, she is going to be mad as a hornet. I'm glad you're here because when she wakes up, I'm using you as a human shield."

I didn't wake up until almost noon. The last time I had looked at the clock was last night at around 6:39. Here it was noon, and I was disoriented. Then I got up and remembered I had a sore ankle. It was red and blue and swollen. Great, I'm not going to fit my fat foot into any of my shoes. I yelled for Jeff with my outside recess voice.

Jacob followed Jeff into my room. Great they seem to be bonding when I'm in pain and I can't enjoy the moment. I had planned to give him an earful, but I saw Jacob's look of concern. "Good grief, how long have I been out? The two of you are buddies now, what year is it, how long was I unconscious? Jeff, I haven't brushed my teeth, or combed my hair, and you thought I'd want to see Jacob now, really?"

"Yes, I did. I thought you would want to kill me, and Jacob might have the power to keep me alive. It's self-preservation Sis. Jacob and I were talking, and he said the day is yours. So, if you need him to help you brush your teeth or comb your hair, he's here for you. I have to make airport runs this afternoon. The cousins have to get back to their homes. Matt left for Washington and Greg left at 5:00 this morning to go back to Ireland."

"Oh no, I didn't get to say good-bye, why didn't someone wake me up? I want to go down and see everyone before they leave."

"I'll help you, Jenna."

"Jeff, tell everyone I'll be downstairs in five, no make that ten minutes. No one gets to leave before I say goodbye."

"Okay."

"I mean it, Jeff, please don't let anyone else leave 'til I get down there."

"Okay Jenna, I'll tell them you'll be right down."

"Jacob, I can't expect you to brush my hair and help me brush my teeth. I can do all that. Just go get my aunt or my mom."

"Jenna. they are helping your Grandma, she's having a rough morning without your grandpa. I'm here let me help you. I'm also carrying you downstairs in nine minutes so you better stand up so I can help you to the bathroom."

"How embarrassing, this just keeps getting better and better, great way to start my day."

"No embarrassment. baby, I love your hair and can't wait to get my fingers in it. I imagined doing this in a different setting, but I'll take what I can get."

"Gentle hands, good to know. How much time do we have left?"

"Believe me not enough time for that. Now, are you ready to say goodbye to your cousins? I'm carrying you downstairs, ready or not, here we come."

He picked me up like I weighed nothing. I don't get guys and their superhuman strength, but I'm loving it at the moment. But, I didn't want my foot to get bumped going down Granny's narrow stairs, so we switched positions to piggy back style, and I have to say I enjoyed the ride. All of a sudden, I was aware I was in a great amount of agony and starving to boot. I'd missed dinner last night and breakfast and it was past lunch. Jacob could read my thoughts before I said anything.

"Jenna. are you hungry? When's the last time you ate something?"

I just shook my head and laughed. "Lunch yesterday, but I power ate because I had big plans for our date night."

"Yeah, how'd that work out for you? Well I'm starving right now so let's eat. How about you when did you eat last, Jacob?"

"It may have been yesterday at lunch for me too."

"Why didn't you eat last night or this morning. Jacob? Are you feeling okay?"

"Why do you think? Because of you, I was worried sick about you. I've felt terrible that you were in pain. You have no earthly idea how you have turned me upside down and inside out. I'm useless. I took the day off to be with you. And don't worry about how many personal or sick days I have available. I'm not a school employee. I will have as many days as we need to be together. Now food, what sounds good?"

"Actually, a grilled cheese sandwich and tomato soup sounds really good right now. And since the cousins are all gone, I hear the local restaurant has great food. Maybe

Alice could wait on us again?"

"If that's what you want, that's what you'll get. Anyone else want a sandwich from town?"

"Jacob, make sure she keeps her foot elevated. Here is another pain pill for her to take with food at lunch. Make sure she takes it with a full glass of water."

"Seriously, Jeff, is it even legal for you to have all these pills?"

"Jacob, I'm a doctor for a living. That's what I do, take care of people. It's who I am, are you getting the picture yet?"

"Yes, I see you have strong protective skills, especially when it comes to your sister. But I'm not going to hurt her, Jeff."

"No, you let your family do that for you. We'll see how well you treat her in time; the jury is still out on that decision."

"Jeff, the accident on the football field was just that, an accident and Andrew feels worse than I do about it. That's low for you to hit below the belt. I love your sister and will take good care of her."

I had to interrupt Jacob and Jeff's banter. "Boys, I need food. Who is taking me out for food?" You would think with all the food people brought, there would be something to eat here, but with a house full for days there wasn't anything that didn't require going to the deep freeze and a lengthy cooking process. "Bye, Granny, see you later."

"Oh, honey, are you going out in public looking like that?" *Didn't take Granny long to get back to her painfully honest comments. Never sugar coating with her.*

Clothes, I was in my sleep wear from last night, and hadn't thought that through. I had a baby blue tee shirt on which left nothing to the imagination and pink and baby blue striped shorts that were shorter than I'd wear out in public for sure!

"No, Granny, Jacob is taking me upstairs and I'm

didn't take time to even open the ketchup packets. Thankfully Jacob opened them for me quickly. I just inhaled them like air. They were all gone by the time we got to Jacob's house. Driving up the long gradual hill, I could see his large, wood, cabin-style home, framed with a wrap-around porch. I loved it! I knew I would love his place. It was classy and strong but not ostentatious. It was country but not backwoods with barns and fences but not clutter, just beautiful.

He came around the truck, opened my door and carried me up the stairs into his house. He sat me on his couch so my leg wouldn't be hanging down, gave me the pill Jeff told him to give me and handed me my Diet Dr. Pepper after I drank a large glass of water. He remembered my drink of choice, good guy this one. I think he's a keeper. I was so self-absorbed with my food I have no idea what Jacob ate. After I had eaten everything in the bag, and drank my drink and Granny's chocolate shake too, oops on that, I was ready to feel human again.

"I want a tour of your place, when you're finished eating of course. I love what I have seen so far. Really, it's so comfortable and stylish. I'm impressed with your find."

"It's not a find, I built it. It took me and my team two years to finish it completely, but it's my home and I'm pleased how everything turned out."

Jacob carried me on my personal tour from room to room saving his master bedroom for the last stop. I had already seen the large open dining room and kitchen from the living room. Off the living room was his office, wooden and masculine with lots of windows. His guest bedroom had a queen bed, dresser and a bathroom off the suite. Off from his kitchen was a pantry room where all the shelves were white and the room was large enough to store a year's worth of food. I guess folks in this area canned their own fruit and vegetables because he had shelves and shelves of fresh canned food. It looked pretty, was organized, colorful and inviting.

His kitchen had stainless steel everything, granite counters, and a gas stove with indoor grill. It was impressive, and I wouldn't change a thing if I had designed it myself. The wooden floors were beautiful, sort of a barn wood looking, warm and strong like my Jacob.

Off the kitchen was a double glass French door that walked out to a large deck holding a table and chairs. Jacob said he goes out there to have his coffee and watch the deer come up in the early morning and at twilight. He said he hand feeds a deer that lost her parent at a young age, he named her Doe.

Off the deck and away from the house is an impressive fire pit with stonework and cement. He said that's where he and his brothers go to have serious talks. If I hear them say, "We need to go to the pit," that's code for I'm coming over, get the hot dogs and marshmallows ready with some cold ones.

Jacob squeezed me in an adoring way. I wanted to kiss him but didn't want to miss seeing anything in his house. I told him he'd better walk faster, because I didn't know how long I could hold back my kisses. He began jogging up the stairs and I laughed. The upstairs had two large rooms. They were empty but had bathrooms attached and then we entered the extra-large master bedroom suite at the end of the hall. I loved every inch of every room. It was comfortable, stylish, and manly. But not manly over the top like having dead animal heads in every room nailed to a wall staring at you. I was thankful for that. It was a dream house created by my dreamboat. *But life is not a dream. And me, I usually find myself rowing up stream against a strong current.*

Jacob gently set me down on his bed. I pushed myself up to where my head was on his pillow and it smelled like my Jacob. I don't know what cologne he wears, but if I wasn't so full, I could have eaten his pillow it smelled so good. Jacob asked me what I was thinking. I told him and he laughed.

"You are so funny."

"Not exactly what I was going for the first time I'm in your bed, but that's sort of how things go for me."

"How are you feeling, babe? That pain pill kicking in yet?"

"It must be because I'm feeling no pain now. I have a full tummy and I'm ready to get to know you up close and personal. Why aren't you on your bed with me right now? This is a big bed and comfy too. Now get over here next to me!"

"We can't do this now. Not when your senses are impaired. I want our first time to be something you'll remember."

"Are you kidding me? I will remember our first time, I promise, it will be memorable. Now get over here with me on your wonderful king-sized bed. I love my Granny, but her beds are like sleeping on a hard-wooden board. Your bed feels like heaven."

"No, Jenna, if I get on that bed with you, we will be naked, and you will regret not waiting until you feel better. We are not doing this now."

"You can't be serious. Come here and just give me a welcome to my house kiss."

"You little tease, you know exactly what your kisses do to me."

"Yep I do, but okay, I'm not going to beg you, or any man for that matter. Carry me out of your den of iniquity. Can we make out on your couch or is that off limits too?"

He raised his eyebrows and gave her a wanting look. "If your foot is elevated, I think we could work around it."

Chapter 12

Disappointment

Jacob once again picked me up and carried me to his living room and his phone rang. Who has a home phone anymore? The answering machine picked up the call and it was playing the message out loud. It was a woman's voice and she seemed very anxious. She was talking so fast I couldn't catch all of what she was saying. Jacob sat me up on his couch and he went to the phone and picked it up. Then he stepped out the kitchen doors onto his deck to take the call, so I couldn't hear the conversation.

He came back inside several minutes later with a forced smile and said, "We should go. We can stop back at Fab food and get your Granny another chocolate malt like she requested; hopefully this one will actually make it all the way to her house."

"Listen, Jacob, if you need to be with someone else, somewhere else right now, I can call Jeff and he can come pick me up on his way back from the airport. I don't want to be an imposition to you."

"No, I have time to stop and get the malt for your Grandma, and get you back to the ranch before I need to deal with a pressing situation. Sorry I need to cut our time short. I was looking forward to several kisses from you. But I do need to take care of certain circumstances."

"Anything you want to share with me? Talk about? Can I help?"

"No nothing for you to worry your pretty little head about, so let's go. You ready to be swept off your feet?"

"Ready and waiting, you know someone up for the job?"

"Baby, your ass better not be in anybody else's arms but mine."

"You've literally got all of me, Jacob, now what are you going to do with me?"

"I've actually given that a lot of thought lately and the possibilities are limitless."

"If that's true, why am I still starving for a kiss from you?"

Jacob smiled his dazzling smile and carried me out the door. He opened the truck door and sat me down on the seat. Not missing a beat, he was on me, kissing with the passion I thought I only felt for him. Things were finally going my way, I was so happy. Finally we were going to be together, in his truck. I can live with that. His boot accidently bumped my ankle and I winced in pain. He immediately lifted off of me, stood up, and held my foot up in the air like it was gold.

"What are you doing?" I said breathlessly. "I'm fine Jacob. We are fine, get back in this truck with me."

"No, I hurt your foot. I know I did. I felt your whole body respond to the pain. And that's with pain meds. You didn't let me know how bad you're hurt. I will not do anything to intentionally hurt you, ever Jenna. We will have a time, a real first second date, and then baby watch out cause you are going to need every ounce of strength you can muster."

"Promises, promises…I'm fine. I'm leaving in a day. I'll be in Missouri and you'll be here in Kentucky. I guess this is best. Just take me to my Granny's house. It sounds like you have another woman who needs a knight in shining armor. Let's get Granny her malt and I'll be out of your hair."

"Jenna, I am not refusing you, or rejecting you. You know that's not how things are with us. I want you more than you can imagine. But our timing is off. You are on pain killers, and you are still in tremendous pain. I can wait. You are worth waiting for, why can't you believe me?"

"Jacob, you should put your seatbelt on, and we can be on our way."

"You put your seatbelt on and then we'll go."

Back at the drive thru Jacob ordered one chocolate malt. "Anything for you, sweetheart."

"Fries, I guess if I can't have sex, I will have to settle for food, small fries, no make that onion rings this time. If you haven't guessed I eat when I'm stressed."

I have no idea why I am so free to talk about sex with Jacob. Seriously we haven't even had a first real date and my body just takes over my mind when I'm with him. This has never happened to me before, ever. I feel like I'm in high school and my hormones are on the intense setting. I don't understand why I feel this way, but he's the best looking man I've ever known, much less kissed. His dark wavy hair is just calling my name. I just want to run my hands through his hair, and grab hold of his strong arms. They are just there begging for me to hold and squeeze them, and his… STOP Jenna, you need to get control of your thoughts, NOW!

"Yes, we'd like two chocolate malts, one onion ring and a large Diet Dr. Pepper. That will be all."

"Why did you get two malts?"

"In case you get the urge for chocolate on the way home

babe, we'll still have your Grandma covered and if not, she can put it in her freezer for a treat later."

"Good thinking, I love a man who can see the big picture and can think ahead. Speaking of thinking ahead, where do you see us, Jacob? What's our future look like to you? Do we even have a future?"

"Tomorrow I'm taking off work and we are having our first real date. Hopefully your ankle will be less swollen and you won't need pills that alter your senses, so we will be free to be together at last."

"That's great, and I'll look forward to that too Jacob, but do you see us beyond tomorrow, when I fly back home?"

"I honestly don't know what's in our future. I've never had a future with a woman before, so I really don't know what we look like. But I know I love you and want to be with you. I don't have all the details worked out in my head yet. No woman has made me feel the way you do. You really did come into my life unexpectedly and I haven't had a thought since our tree swinging kiss that hasn't included you. I don't know how you got under my skin but that's the truth. It's like you are a part of me, you are in my heart."

"Wow, Jacob, your words are so powerful to me. Thank you for being so honest about your feelings."

We pulled into Granny's driveway way too soon. "Jacob, you have mad skills with building and wood working and your house is amazing. I loved every nail and piece of wood in your home. I mean that. You should be very proud of your masterpiece."

"Thanks, Jenna. I love that house too. It is me. I'm at home and comfortable there. Let me ask you a serious question for a minute. Do you think you could feel at home and comfortable there in my home if it were our home, in time you know, down the road?"

"I guess time will have to tell. I think happiness is a choice we make and the only person who can make you happy is you. I'm a pretty positive and happy person,

Jacob. Sorry I've been so needy with a funeral and then my foot injury. I'm usually a lot more fun."

"I don't want to keep you. I heard that woman's voice on the phone and she sounded upset. I didn't mean to eavesdrop on your conversation, but what I heard sounded like a woman in need."

"I really hate to leave you right now, but something did come up and I've got to go. I'll call you or come by later this afternoon if that's okay?"

"Why don't you call first, and I'll see what's going on. Are you ready to carry me to the door?"

"Ready."

"Before you carry me to the house can I have our goodbye kiss out here, now?"

"Jenna, I'm coming back. I'll see you later. But sure, I'll take whatever invitations I can get to be closer to you. Pucker up baby because here I come."

"Man, I'm going to miss your kisses Jacob. I'm sorry Partner died, but I'm so glad you came into my life. You are an amazing man. I really care for you and wish you the best, always."

"Okay, Jenna, to the house. You are talking about goodbyes and we still have our first date tomorrow."

"Yeah, well we had it scheduled for two days ago, then one day ago, then today and it always gets moved to some day in the future. What if tomorrow never comes for us?"

"Jenna, all this tomorrow's never coming stuff is the pain pills talking. Babe, go take a nap, and I'll call you later this afternoon."

He carried me into the house. Jeff, my mom, aunt, uncles and Granny are sitting in the den. The TV was on, but no one was watching. I'm pretty sure they were waiting for me to get home. Jeff thanked Jacob for Granny's malt, and I curled up with an ice pack on my ankle and a blanket in Granny's rocking chair. The blanket smelled like Partner's old spice cologne. I was listening to their conversation and sometime, somehow, once again, I fell asleep. I woke up and my ankle felt like it was going to explode it was so tight and full of pressure.

"Jeff, can you look at my ankle, it really hurts. I don't think it should hurt worse now than it did when I twisted it, or is that how it heals?"

"Sis, I told you we should have gone to the hospital when it happened. X-rays are the only way I have to know what's going on with your foot. If you are in pain, let me take you to the hospital and we can check things out and see what's going on. You'll feel better and so will I. Let me call the hospital and talk to a few people first then I'll drive you there."

"Granny, will you be okay? Dwayne, Thomas, Elaine and Mom are still here for you. We are just going to run to town and check my ankle."

"We'll be fine, darling. Sweet, Jeff, you take Jenna to town and tell them you're my Grandson."

"Okay, Granny. Don't worry, we won't be long. We'll call before we leave to see if you need anything from town before we head back."

Mom wanted to go with us, but Granny wanted her to stay with her. She knew I'd be fine with Dr. Jeff by my side.

"Yep, Sis, your x-rays are back, and your ankle is broken. Now for the really bad news. You ready for this? We have to re-break your ankle to set it in the correct position and then we need to put you in a cast so you can heal properly. By the way, you need more calcium in your diet Jenna because your bone density is too brittle. That typically happens when women start getting a certain age."

"Really, Jeff? You think it's a good time to knock a girl when she's down with the age card? I'm not that old and I'm also younger than you!"

"Jenna, you may be down, but not out. You are a fighter, you have it in your blood. Your ankle should heal just fine.

Now, tell me about you and Jacob? Is this going to last beyond this weekend or what's going on?"

"Nice job getting my mind off my ankle. Jeff, I honestly don't know about Jacob and me. I've fallen for Jacob, and he's amazing. You should see his house. He designed and built it. I think if you gave him a real chance you would really like him. He is very affectionate, a good kisser and, Jeff..."

"Jenna, stop right there. You are on strong pain killers right now and just don't finish that sentence about you and lover boy Jacob. Let me help you walk to the car. We don't want Granny to worry. Otherwise you know she will be sending you a letter about your behavior and overall klutziness. You know Granny loves writing us her handwritten letters."

"Okay, take me to Granny's. I'm so tired, I don't know why, but I could use a nap. Hey, have I thanked you for buying me a ticket so I could be here. That was so sweet of you. I really appreciate it more than you know. Love you, Bro."

"Love you too, Sis, now sit back and take a nap while I get you back to Granny's."

"Why is everyone so concerned about me eating and napping? I can do just fine on my own."

"Yes, you're the bomb, Sis; you are the bomb, night, night."

I woke up three hours later and felt like a new woman. I don't remember getting out of the car and going into Granny's house. I woke up in bed with a cast on my foot. I had different pain killers that didn't make me so hungry. I hated feeling like I wanted to eat the bark off trees, and my ankle didn't really hurt that bad anymore. Things were looking up. I guess the cast helped. J   Jeff   is   leaving tomorrow and wants me to go with him so he can help me with my suitcases and get home safe and sound. It makes sense. He changed his flight then he's renting a car and driving from my place in Missouri to his place in Kansas. He misses his wife and boys and I wish they could have been here too, but I was full-time needy this weekend and he was full-time helpful. So glad he cleared his schedule to be there for me, mom, Granny, and the rest of the family. Love my big brother so much.

We live about four hours away from each other, but with his busy lifestyle, and my lack of funds, we don't get together very often and that is the sad truth of our relationship. Thank goodness for unlimited minutes on our cell plans. I love his wife, she's like the sister I never had. We have great times together. I miss her and my nephews too.

With me leaving early, how am I going to tell Jacob we don't get our long-awaited date? I miss him already and I haven't even said goodbye. I have to pull up my big girl panties, make the call, and tell him goodbye.

"Jacob, hi, this is Jenna. I hate to leave this on a phone message, but I'm flying back home tomorrow. Jeff is going to fly home with me and help me with my luggage and transportation. I hate that we don't get our date together, but that just gives me something to look forward to in our future. If this is goodbye, then thank you for everything Jacob. You made me feel alive when I didn't think that would ever happen for me. So, thanks for the hugs and kisses and carrying me around for two days. I miss you already. Bye my, Jacob."

Jacob didn't call me that night. He said he'd call or come by, but he didn't do either. Maybe I didn't remember the conversation we'd had correctly, with the pain meds, but I hope that desperate woman who called him is alright. I hope it wasn't Ms. Ruth. Maybe I should call her and tell her goodbye too.

"Hello, Ms. Ruth, this is Jenna Lee. I just wanted to let you know I'm going back earlier than expected and how great it was to see you and your family while I was here."

"Jenna, it was great to see you again too. How's your ankle?"

"Well I went to the hospital today and it was broken. I'm getting along much better with a cast instead of hopping around like a rabbit. Your Jacob was a saint to tote me around this week. I will miss his company."

"Well he's done nothing but talk about you since he saw you standing in my parlor. Don't you worry about your Grandma, Jenna. When all your family has gone, I'll make sure one of my boys or hired hands goes by and checks on her every day. I will let you know if there is anything noteworthy about your Grandmother. We take care of our own around these parts."

"Thank you, that means the world to me. Ms. Ruth, I can't seem to connect with Jacob to tell him goodbye personally, but if you would let him know I tried to get in touch with him, I would appreciate it."

"Consider it done, my sweet little Jenna. If you need anything, dear, you call Ms. Ruth and I will make sure things are handled. I consider you unlucky in flag football, but brilliant in the areas that count in life. It was wonderful seeing you again. Travel safe and don't worry about your Grandma."

We had dinner and I went upstairs to pack. Granny's kids were all going to stay on a few days to make sure all the paperwork, and legal stuff was transferred over into the proper names, and that Granny was going to adjust to being alone. They are working on schedules so they can take turns coming out to stay with Granny. Granny is a home body, and everyone knows she won't leave her beloved farm to come visit her kids and grandkids. She didn't leave the farm with Partner, so now we all know she won't leave now that Partner is gone. Everyone had to make plans to come and help her.

I wish I knew what happened to Jacob and if he's okay, but I guess I just have to let him go and enjoy what we had, whatever I was to him. He made me feel special, beautiful, and desired. That's something I haven't felt in many years. I will miss being the center of attention by someone I was attracted to more than I've ever desired another man in my life.

That's it. He must secretly be a werewolf or a vampire and it's a full moon tonight so he couldn't come out without risking my safety. I'm sure that must be the reason for no response. Well tomorrow, I'm gone, and he will just be a memory, a dream that dissolved when I woke.

Chapter 13

Airport Drama

At the airport, the security guard asked me to take off my cast. Are they kidding? He said he needed to check for drugs and that was the only way because the x-ray machine can't see through my cast.

"I haven't even had my cast on for 24 hours and you want me to take it off? This cast isn't coming off anytime soon. I can't even get it wet. Talk to my doctor, he's also my brother, who is traveling with me."

Jeff was standing behind me holding his sides laughing. He had told the security guy, apparently a friend from the past, to tell me that just to see what I'd do and say. That's what I get for leaving him alone for five minutes to go to the bathroom. They were both laughing and giving high fives to each other like they were best friends for life. Where did Jeff find this guy?

"Really, Jeff, you thought I needed this now? Boys! Jeffery Scott, that was not funny."

At that comment and by me saying his full name like when he'd get in trouble when we were little, his laughter erupted into a full volume roar as we are motioned to go through the body scanner and move on to the plane. As I am going through the scanner, I hear his voice. It's Jacob and he's calling out my name.

"Jenna, wait, Jenna WAIT!"

I stopped, turned around, and saw my Jacob jogging toward me. I left my carry-on bag sitting on the floor where it stood and my shoe in the scanner bucket. I ran straight toward him, cast on one-foot, bare foot with the other. The problem was I forgot there was a Plexiglass wall between us, and I ran smack into it. Being that it was transparent, Jacob had a full and a clear view of the whole crash incident. How he held in his laughter is beyond me, but I could hear Jeff laughing so hard he was snorting behind me. I just ignored him. By the time Jacob made it around the Plexiglass wall to get to me, I was rubbing my nose to stop my eyes from watering. He just shook his head.

"Jenna, it's never boring with you, it's always the unexpected. Babe, you are like an accident waiting to happen. How did you not see a wall?"

"Well, Jacob, I knew past a certain point they wouldn't let you in without a ticket, and my plane is boarding, so I wanted to give you a chance to, to say goodbye. I wasn't thinking about my surroundings, I just wanted to get to you."

What I really wanted to say was I wanted to give you a chance to let me know where you have been and why you blew me off, but I didn't want to sound needy. I really hate insecure needy women and I hate that I feel like one right now.

"Jenna, I was in my truck in the rolling hills of Kentucky and I was in dead zones with my phone. I ran over some nails on the highway and blew three of my tires. I had to walk miles before I could get phone reception.

Then it was very late, and I didn't want to wake you. I couldn't reach you on your phone this morning, guess it was since you were at the airport there was connection problems. It kept going to voice mail. My Grandma told me you called. I didn't get your message until I was headed back from my Grandma's and she told me you'd left. Our date Jenna, you cancelled our date?"

"I'm sorry I didn't want to, but that's the way it worked out."

"Just because I didn't return your call, you leave early?"

"No, that's not the reason. My brother is helping me get home, so I had to go when it was best for him. He wants to get home and be with his family."

"Jenna, you are in a cast! I knew you were in pain. What's wrong with your ankle? Is it broken?"

"Yes, but honestly it's much better now that it's reset and in a cast. I don't move it around or bump it by accident."

"Yeah, that scenario I'm familiar with. Well, Jenna, I'm going to miss you. Can I kiss you goodbye?"

"Come here." I whispered in his ear, "I came to your house, now it's your turn to come to mine. Call me. We can make this work, if you want us to work. I've got to get on that plane, so Jacob, kiss me goodbye."

Jacob kissed me with longing passion and even the toes on my broken ankle curled under in sheer delight. If I was such a wet noodle after a passionate kiss, I would never live through one round of making love with him. I'd die on the table, in the truck, in the bed, wherever it may be, my body would surely die. I love him, I do. Should I say it out loud? No, I'm leaving. No tears, Jenna. Just one more kiss and turn and walk away.

He didn't let me get another word out. He grabbed my rear end and pulled my face up to his face. My legs were locked around his waist and it would have taken the jaws-of-life to pull us apart. Jeff called my name.

"Jenna, we have to go!"

Jacob whispered in my ear, "Jenna, I'm coming to your house soon for our first, second, third, fourth, and fifth dates. I think I love you. I really do Jenna. I already miss you and you aren't even gone yet."

He just told me he loves me.

"Jacob, after our first, second, third, fourth, and fifth dates, you won't have to think you love me, you'll know." With a smile I turned and walked to Jeff.

Jeff just shook his head. "So long, Jacob."

"Jeff…be safe. Jenna until we meet again."

And with that, Jeff and I were on the plane and waiting for takeoff. There was no upgrade to first class this trip home, but I got the window and Jeff got the aisle in the two-seat row we were sitting in. It was a pleasant trip home. The man I love told me he thinks he loves me. I think I love him too. What am I going to do? How will I manage for days on end without him?

"Excuse me, stewardess, I'm going to need fries, do you have fries? Okay, chips will have to do then, and a Diet Dr. Pepper, please, as soon as possible. I'm dealing with grief."

After the snack, I was off in my recent pastime of taking a nap. Jeff is on his phone texting and working on his laptop, so I just closed my eyes and we were back in Missouri in no time.

After we landed, Jeff and I went to dinner together then he took me home. He grabbed a couple of bottles of water, a baggie of cheese sticks and pretzels, and gave me a hug. He was on his way home.

"Thanks Jeff, for going out of your way for me. I'm so proud to have you as my brother. Please drive safe and if you get tired, call me and I'll talk to you till you make it home. Pinky swear you'll do that?"

"Okay, love you too. I'm fine Jenna. See you probably next at mom's on Thanksgiving but we'll see what happens between now and then."

"Give your wife and the boys my love. Thank them for sharing you with me. Love ya, Bro!"

"Love you too, Sis."

As soon as he left, I called mom to talk to her and Granny. "We made it to my place safe and sound, and Jeff is on the road as we speak. He should be home in four to five and a half hours. He promised if he gets tired, he'll call me but I'm sure he'll be fine. He is in home mode and his brain is going a mile a minute."

"Jacob just left the farm," Granny said. "He'd stopped by to make sure I was doing okay. He said he missed you already. You always did know how to make an impression, Jenna."

Great now I'm for sure going to get a long, long letter from Granny, with Jacob as the main topic. I can tell from the tone in her voice.

"Thanks, Granny. I'll talk to you later, love you, goodbye."

Chapter 14

Alone Again

I'm home a day earlier than expected. Now I have time to do my laundry and play with my dogs. I felt sad, melancholy, I couldn't smell Jacob anymore. I couldn't feel his hand holding mine, touching me. I couldn't feel his gentle warm whisper making the hairs on my neck stand at full attention. I missed his strong manly voice, firm and commanding, but never cruel or harsh. I missed the man I fell in love with at my Grandfather's funeral. How is such a thing possible? How can I go back to my ordinary life with him not by my side? I miss my Jacob. When will he call me? If I'm out of sight will I be out of his mind too? How is it that I can't think a thought without it reminding me of him?

If he'd have asked me to stay with him in Kentucky, I think I would have, just to be in close proximity to him. For my Jacob, I would have stayed. How ridiculous is that? One weekend with a man and I'm ready to change my entire life? But he didn't ask me to stay and now being at home seems empty and lonely. I'm not even happy in my happy home anymore. I hear Moose, my puggle, snoring on the couch by my side, and I wonder if Jacob snores when he sleeps. Honestly if I can sleep through Moose's snoring, I think I can deal with Jacob's.

I'm calling Jacob. I called and it went to voice mail. I hate leaving a voice mail, I want to have a conversation with this man. Great, now I have to say something intelligent. "Hello, Jacob, I just wanted you to know I made it home safe and sound and I miss you. Your smile, your voice, your touch, I miss you. Take care of yourself, Jacob, bye."

I hung up the phone and had to choke back tears. Enough, Jenna, get yourself together! That's it, I'm not calling him again. I never know what to say on a voice mail. Then he can replay over and over my message and laugh at what a dork I am. I'm not calling him again. Jenna, do you hear yourself? You are not going to humiliate yourself on another phone message to Jacob. That was it.

Okay just think about work, I miss my kindergarteners. They will keep me busy, purposeful and challenged. I can't wait for Monday. I should go to school tomorrow and get things organized from my time away and read the notes from my substitute.

Maybe I'll go to a church tomorrow. I used to go every Sunday but haven't gone much at all since my divorce. I don't think I told Jacob I'm divorced. So many conversations we haven't had together. I wonder if we will ever get that chance to share our thoughts, fears, and hopes for the future. Do I have a future with him? I guess time will tell if he contacts me or not. I'm rambling in my own thoughts, I can't keep them straight in my head, and they are all over the board. I need to focus on something besides Jacob. Maybe I should bake a cake, or make some cookies? Chocolate chip or peanut butter? Hum, I like the cookie dough best anyway, so chocolate chip here we go.

The phone rang and I jumped. "Hello? Jacob? Oh honey, it's so good to hear your voice, I'm so glad you called me."

"Jenna, sweetheart, when's the next time you are off from work?"

"It won't be until the next holiday. Why?"

"I want to book a flight and come see you, but I don't want to wait that long."

"Good, I don't want to wait that long to see you either, so when are you coming?"

"How about next week, is that too soon for you? Do you need more time to recover with your broken ankle?"

"No, come see me. Come be with me. I miss you so much!"

"I can't erase any of your messages from my phone. I listen to your voice and I'm rendered totally dysfunctional. I can't do anything but think of you and wish I was, well, let's just say, wish I was with you."

"Jacob, are you really coming to see me or is this going to be like one of our wishful date nights?"

"Absolutely count on it, baby, I'm coming. If you are inviting me to come, I'm getting the ticket as soon as I'm off the phone with you."

"Jacob, sweetheart, can you afford to miss work for a week? You took off time to take care of me last week, are you sure it's okay?"

"I don't need permission to live my life. I'm my own boss, I make the rules for my life, and my livelihood isn't in danger darling. So, rest easy. I will call you when I get my ticket arrangements finalized, then we can have an entire week together."

"Jacob, I just had a terrible thought. I was just off a week for Partner's funeral and I won't be able to take off time when you're here. Have you been to Missouri before?"

"No, but you can 'show me' the sights. Get it, Missouri

is the show me state. I can't wait for you to show me your many sights. I'm coming to see you. I could care less about Missouri, babe. Don't feel like you need to entertain me. I can bring my laptop and work while you're at work."

"You could come see me tomorrow, it wouldn't be too soon for me. A week is so long to be apart. I miss you terribly."

"I'll buy my ticket and get business matters ready for me to be off a week, and that way I can really be with you and give you my full attention. Maybe it might be better for me to just get in my truck and drive to Missouri?"

"No, Jacob, that's such a long drive to make and all by yourself. Just take the time you need. A week isn't that long to wait for us to be together. Fly to Springfield, Branson, Kansas City, or Oklahoma and I'll pick you up at whatever airport gives you the best last-minute pricing. I need you safe and sound. I can wait one week. I will miss you every minute we aren't together, but I will wait. I'm hanging up so you can make plane reservations now. I will pick you up at the airport and you can stay with me, only if you're not opposed to staying with me and my two roommates, Molly and Moose. I warn you Moose snores."

"I am all in. One week will seem like an eternity; but, my love, in just one week we will be together. I love you, Jenna. I really do. If a man tells a woman he loves her and there has been no sex prior to the 'I love you,' then you can take that to the bank baby. It's the gospel truth."

"Jacob, I'm hopelessly in love with you too. I'm under your spell. I can't think clearly, and I miss you every minute we are apart. I feel, well I'll show you how I feel when you get here."

"You have no idea of my many feelings for you. Until our dates, you'll just have to visit me in your dreams."

"You're such a romantic, so suave and debonair, so charming and irresistible, even on the phone. There has to be something majorly wrong with you that I just don't know yet, because you are too good to be true. Do you have or have you had any mental illness, done prison time? What am I missing here?"

"Oh, Jenna, you are so funny. Babe, it's getting late and you need your rest. Stay healthy, and don't run into any walls or break any more bones. I will call my travel agent as soon as we hang up and I'll get my tickets. I'll call you tomorrow and let you know when I'll arrive and on which flight."

"Okay, sweet dreams my love."

"Love you too, babe, I'll call you tomorrow."

I couldn't stop smiling. Tomorrow will be myself-prepping day. Pedicure, manicure, pluck my eyebrows, haircut, maybe just a trim, he likes my long hair. Clean my house so everything's done before he gets here. I can wait a week, it's only seven days. I've waited a lifetime for my dreams to come true, what's one week? He loves me and he's coming to see me. He wants to know me in a biblical sense. I can't wait to finally be with the hottest, sexiest man I've ever seen.

I'm back at work with my kids and my days go by expeditiously. I tutor after school so it's 7:00 p.m. before I get home anyway. He said he'd call after I got home so I'm paying attention when I drive. He might ask me what I ate today, not sure why food is an issue, but I guess it shows that he cares about me and wants me to be healthy. What did I eat today? Let me think, Diet Dr. Pepper for breakfast, Smart Ones frozen dinner for lunch, and nothing for dinner yet. Find something Jenna, coffee for now and I'll find something to eat after I talk with Jacob. I'm not really hungry and that's not like me usually, but I've been so busy I haven't had an appetite.

It was 7:30 p.m. and my phone rang. Jacob's number

registered on my phone "A boyfriend, Jacob". I need to get his picture so when he calls, I can see his handsome face. Put that on my to-do list for when he gets here.

"Hi, babe, what are you doing?"

"Waiting for your call, how was your day, sweetheart?"

"Long. Listen my flight will be at the Springfield Airport on Thursday at 5:00 p.m., will that work for you?"

"Yes, yes, yes. Thursday at 5:00. I'll be the woman at the airport with a mattress tied to her back."

"Ha, that's my girl, Jenna."

"Yes, I talk very bravely when you are hundreds of miles away. I would think those things but probably never say them out loud if you were here."

"So, what you're telling me is that I'm in love with a crazy woman?"

"Yes, you found me out, crazy in love with you."

"Babe, I've got massive amounts of work to do and I'm still at the office so I can take off a week. If you are sure that will work for your schedule, then I'll see you Thursday evening. I love you, Jenna."

"I love you too, Jacob. Miss me while we are apart."

"I heard a line in a chick flick movie once that I thought was nonsense but after meeting you, I can say that line knowing full well it sounds bizarre, but I mean this… "I think I would miss you even if we had never met, Jenna."

"Oh my gosh, I know that movie too. I think it's from *The Wedding Date*, or something like that. Baby I feel the same way. I can't wait to hold your hand, to feel your breath on my skin, the taste of your lips... I can't go on because I've never done phone sex before and I don't want our first sexual experience to have a phone anywhere in that scene."

Laughing, Jacob says, "Okay, until Thursday I'll have you in my dreams too. Love you, babe."

"Love you too, my Jacob."

I got off the phone and started dancing around the room.

My dogs were running in circles wondering what was wrong with me. He loves me and I love him. What comes next? Sex! *Finally, a physically hot off the charts man is going to see me naked. Hmmm, I didn't think this through.*

I need to buy soft lights for the bedroom, maybe remove all light bulbs and just have candles? No, I have dogs, a possible fire hazard, what was I thinking? Oh, I know, I wasn't thinking.... I didn't think this through. What am I going to do? He's paid a lot of money to take off work and fly out to spend an entire week with me, just me. He has high expectations and he's going to see me naked.

This may not turn out like the dream that's been in my heart and mind. I'm sure he's seen many beautiful women naked, and now it's me, not in the same hotness category as him. What am I going to do? He was engaged to a literal model. This is not going to turn out well for me. There is no way I can compete with model perfection.

I only have a week I don't have time to join a gym. I guess I could go to a tanning booth. If I can't be thinner and fit then tanner would help my glow in the dark white skin not look so fat. I have to look thinner, feel thinner. I could go every night, maybe once before school and once after work. Calling tanning booths now, check the hours open. Yep, that's what I will have to do.

What will I do if he gets here, and sees me naked and isn't attracted to me anymore? How will I live with that rejection? What if he changes his mind, and doesn't want me at all? Here I am, the Jenna I know, who looks and thinks about things from every angle before acting like a fool. But this is Jacob I'm talking about, and I am going to hope that I kiss him good enough to temporarily blind him to what I look like naked.

I don't want to think this out in every situation. I want to be surprised, swept off my feet. And even if it's just one time, one night, I'm not going to regret being with this amazingly sexy man. I'm sure he's not stressing out about being intimate with me, so I'm not going to get all self-conscience about being with the hottest man I've ever seen. I'm just going to love this man in every way I can and if it's not enough for him, at least I let him know how I felt.

I can only be honest, and I do want to be with him more than I've wanted anyone or anything ever. I can't wait until he's here. I miss his manly voice. I loved the strength of his rugged man hands holding me. It made me feel so strong, so taken care of. How crazy is that to feel this way? I've been married before and to have these feelings for another man is so unexpected. I'm so happy I don't have to be alone anymore. God help me and Jacob be the happily ever after I've always dreamed could be possible.

Chapter 15

The First (Second) Date

The girls at work will think I've made up some mythical creature named Jacob. He really does sound too good to be true even for me and I know he's real. You would think working in an elementary school all the teachers would be really nice and supportive for each other. But things are complicated at my school.

In an educational climate, teachers used to share ideas and resources. But now, pay raises are based on how well your individual class scores on district and state mandated tests, many teachers no longer share and collaborate anymore. Everyone is competing against one another and there are even teachers being dishonest on student scores, so they get their raise based on performance results. This merit pay sounds good in the news and in the business world, but it isn't best for kids in the academic world. Basically put, teachers work hard; they should just be paid for their education, dedication and quality of work.

The school district only has so much money to share evenly with each school, therefore, not all teachers get their hard-earned raises. So who gets the raises? When too many teachers got high scores from their students, the principal picks his/her friends to get the pay increases. It's so sad how poor choices at the political level have created this toxic environment for teachers to work around.

As far as my professional life, I just try to live my life, and focus on my responsibilities. I have many good girl friends that are co-workers and we laugh together almost every day.

My happy thoughts drift back to Jacob. I wonder how can people that work with me on a daily basis, not notice the new excitement I have growing in me every day as it gets closer to Thursday. My Jacob will be here soon, and I can't make myself stop smiling. I've cancelled my after school tutoring lessons for Thursday. I've shaved my legs and checked the paint job on my toenails, which still looked great from my pedicure just days earlier. My manicure still looks beautiful too. I cleaned my house, filled my car with gas, and bought candles for the bath and bedroom. I'm ready to pick up my Jacob. I'm so excited to finally see him. It's only been a week, but it seems like months ago when I saw him last.

Thursday at 4:01 I left school and headed directly to the airport; did not pass go, did not collect $200.00. My car was washed and cleaned inside. I wore a cute baby chick yellow dress with coral and pink little flowers all over it. My tanning sessions have paid off and you can tell I'm looking good, if I do say so myself. I don't think Jacob's ever seen me in a dress before. I don't even look too bad with my cast accessory. I'm going to see my Jacob in 30 minutes and counting. I can't believe how happy he makes me, and we aren't even in the same state yet.

Seriously Jenna, what are you doing? I don't want to analyze this from every angle, but I feel like I'm not being responsible if I don't. Part of me, my largest parts just want to love him and enjoy our time together, that's it, that's all there is, that's all I want. But my mind won't shut off. It keeps saying Jenna slow down, what's the rush? Think things out before you do anything stupid. Don't get physical, get to know him first. Talk to him and see him in different settings. Pay attention to how he acts in different situations. Don't make the same mistakes you did before.

All of this inner monologue in my head, no wonder I have to turn it off or I'd go crazy. Why do I have this turmoil? Why can't I just let myself enjoy the moment for what it is? A beautiful man wants to love a nice middle-aged woman. All the childhood training about waiting until you're married, well it's not like I can go back in time to be a virgin again, so I just have to trust myself and hope I make better choices this time. I just want to be happy and to make Jacob happy. That oldies song, if loving you is wrong, I don't want to be right, is at the front of my mind right now. But…no Jenna just stop it! Jacob's made the big gesture. He's taken off a week of work, flown out to my state, to do what? To see me, just me and to have our first second date. Enjoy this gift of a man Jenna, allow yourself to be happy and appreciate his company. Don't be so judgmental, just be in the moment and enjoy your life.

Sharply at 4:29, I was at the airport luggage pick up area, waiting to embrace my long-awaited Kentucky man. I've checked the vicinity for any Plexiglass between me and the walkway to where Jacob would be entering the room, so I wouldn't embarrass myself like I did the last time I saw him. Then I heard a man calling my name, but it wasn't Jacob's voice. Who in the world could that be?

"Jenna, Jenna Lee is that you?"

"Yes, it's me. Is that you, Scott Beck?"

"You remembered me too, how long it has been, since high school?"

"Scott, it is so good to see you, it's been forever!"

Scott rushed up to me and gave me a big hug. He was always a handsome man. He was tall, had sandy blond hair, and thin. I was so shocked to see my old friend that I temporarily forgot about Jacob. Scott was hugging me, lifting me up in the air and I was suddenly very aware that my dress was shorter than I thought and drafty when I was being spun around in a circle. Then I saw Jacob as I was being twirled in the air.

"Scott, Scott, you have to put me down. I'm really glad to see you too, and I'd love to catch up, but I'm meeting someone and I see him now."

I peeled myself away from Scott and hated to say goodbye, because I didn't end things with Scott the way I wish I had years ago. But my Jacob was here, and I couldn't wait to see him.

Jacob was not smiling at me, not even a forced grin. He was glaring at me, then at Scott. Scott was checking out Jacob from what I could see out the corner of my eye. I went to throw my arms around Jacob and he said in a cold tone, "Apparently all my hopes of grabbing you and swinging you in joyous rapture have already been done, so I guess a simple hello will have to do for now."

"Jacob, Scott's an old friend I haven't seen since high school. He was the first guy to like me, so snap out of it! I'm so glad to see you Jacob, aren't you even going to give me a kiss?"

"Yeah, baby, I'll kiss you when I get over my internal jealous rage. Give me a minute or two, Jenna."

"Fine then, let's stand over here and wait for your luggage."

While waiting for his luggage, Jacob isn't talking to me, and Scott walks over to visit. Great, I have no boyfriend for years then two men at one time at the same place want all my attention. Oh brother. I thought while Jacob is cooling down, I could take advantage of the time and visit with my old friend.

"Jenna, do you remember my sister Shelley?" Scott asked.

"Sure, how is she?"

"Well not so good. I am just coming home from her husband Randy's funeral. She has two grown sons and they are staying with her for a while until she's doing a little better. It was a farming accident. It's hard to adjust to those life changes when they happen so unexpectedly."

"I'm so sorry, Scott. Shelley was always so beautiful and fun to be with. I remember high school days and her dating Randy and me spending the night with her, talking all night. Please let her know I wish her the best. Now tell me about you, how are things with you?"

"I'm still married to Judy. We have two daughters, Lisa and Kim. They are both in college, one working on her masters and the other just graduated. I own a trucking company and drive big rigs. I don't like being inside working at a desk, so my wife runs the office and keeps all my drivers in line. How about you Jenna? Where has life taken you? How's your folks and brother?"

"Well ... Oh, I see the luggage is here. Maybe we can catch up another time?"

"Here, let me have your phone number and I'll check with Judy to schedule a time we can meet in Kansas City or St. Joe and have dinner, go dancing and catch up on old times."

"That sounds great, it is so good to see you! Tell your mom Nelda, hello for me too."

Jacob must have heard Scott mention the word wife or noticed that Scott was wearing a wedding ring because the color quickly came back into his handsomely rugged cheeks. He stepped forward and pulled his luggage off the conveyer belt. I gave Scott a hug goodbye. Jacob grabbed me around the waist, pulled me to him, and kissed me until I thought I'd lose all my dignity and composure.

We walked to my SUV and put his suitcase in the back.

"What are you hungry for, Jacob?"

"You, baby, just you."

"No way, you are going to need all your strength for what I have planned for you, so if you don't have any food requests, I'll just pick a place."

"You choose, I'm with you, remember this is your town."

"Yes, you are with me, for an entire week! If I forget to tell you later, thank you, Jacob, for coming to see me. I had a wonderful time. You are amazing."

Jacob just sported a sexy smile and a look in his eyes I could have drowned in. "Now for food, I've never had a bad steak at the Texas Roadhouse, so how about there for an early dinner? And it's on the way to my house too."

"That sounds great, let's go. Wait a minute, Jenna, do you want me to drive? I didn't realize you had a stick shift transmission. How are you getting around with a cast on your leg and using a clutch? That is terrible, why didn't you tell me?"

"It has been very difficult to get around. I've actually had a couple of close calls driving this week, but you make things work when you have no other options."

"Okay, you can be a passenger seat driver, telling me where to go and how to get there. It will be like we are a real married couple."

"Ha, ha!"

"Seriously I'll drive us to dinner if that's okay with you. No GPS?"

"No, they didn't even have GPS options back when I bought this in 1999."

"Okay, you tell me the directions and we will work as a team."

"I like the sound of that, it's like music to my ears. Jacob, I love you, I really love you. It doesn't make sense to me, this is all so sudden, so totally out of my comfort zone, foreign to my rational thought, but my emotions are real, and I honestly love you. I'm not just saying that to get you to say it back to me, I just adore you and I'm so glad you are here with me. Thank you for coming, sweetheart."

"Jenna, I've never been more jealous or full of rage than when I was at the airport and I saw some man hugging and swinging my girl in circles. By the way, thanks for wearing your red thong for me. Do you have the red bra on too?"

"How did you know? Scott, I'm going to kill him! And yes, I'm wearing them both for you. Only for you Jacob and sorry for the pre-show, that was unexpected."

We finally arrived at the restaurant and with only one missed turn. I was talking and forgot to tell Jacob to turn left. We ordered, Jacob got prime rib, baked potato with butter and sour cream and a side salad, and I got my standard filet mignon that was flavorful and tender. My baked sweet potato and salad was tasty too. But after eating my entire plate, I couldn't wait to get Jacob to my house.

As we were headed to my place, I wanted to set the stage, so Jacob isn't disappointed. "Jacob, my house isn't grand like your home, but it's in a safe neighborhood. It has two bedrooms, two baths, an office, attached garage, and a fenced backyard for my dogs. It has everything I need. So please don't compare my house to yours, because I'm not a builder and don't have the funds you do to build or buy."

"It was a safe and affordable place for me to live after my divorce. I was new to the area and this house has been a healing place for me. It needs new carpet, painting, landscaping, but you know what, I don't stress over all the things I don't have or can't afford. I just appreciate what I've got. It's a home that I'm free to be myself in, my own house. You have no idea what a joy that is to feel free in my own home, I can just be me. I hope you can appreciate it like I do."

"Do you want to have the funds to build or buy something else? I'll help you if you want a different house. We can look while I'm here."

"No way, Jacob, I'm not poor teacher Jenna. I'm being honest with you, telling you my private things, not for you to feel sorry for me and be Mr. Moneybags. Jacob, I don't need your money, I don't need rescued, I just need you. Your money doesn't make me happy. You alone make me happy. I just don't want you to be disappointed with my house, because it's been here, where I've come back from the dead."

"Sorry I snapped at you just now, but this trip is for us to enjoy one another not to do home improvement projects. Unless you are one of those men that really enjoy that sort of thing? I'll do whatever you would enjoy doing. The week is ours. I just want to spend as much time as possible with you in any way and every way I can."

Chapter 16

The Surprise

Here we are, Jacob, it's the next house on the left. I know it's not brick, but the siding is nice dark gray color. My burgundy shutters and gray flecked roof sort of frames it don't you think? Let me go around and let you in the front door so you can see it from the entryway for a good first impression. Like a guest would see it, and not through my garage and laundry room. Oh, and just a warning, my dogs are a little hyper when they first meet someone, but after a few minutes they calm down to their normal loveable selves. Molly is the fawn or tan haired girl and Moose is the bigger black colored boy puggle. You can put your luggage in my guest bedroom."

"Are you planning on me sleeping in the guest bedroom?"

"It's an option we can discuss later."

"It's your place, I'll go and do what you want me to do."

"Jacob, I want you to take me, take all of me. I want you

to make love to me. But if you're tired, jet lagged or too full, I will understand. I've worked all day, had a large meal and I'm tired too, so there is no pressure for us to make something happen tonight. Let me give you my home tour. I'll save my bedroom for last like you did at your place for me, remember?"

"This is my living room and dining room and it's open to my kitchen." We didn't even make it down the hall before his hands were under my dress, on my butt cheeks, lifting me up to his body. My legs instinctively wrapped around his waist and we walked past each door until he got to the last room, my bedroom. "Is this our room baby?"

"Yes", I said already breathless. "The dogs need to be put into their kennels, or they will think you are attacking me and they might try to bite you."

"Have your dog's seen a lot of this behavior before?"

"No of course not, but my dogs are protective of me. You are the first man I've had in my bed."

"Why wouldn't your dogs be protective of you, man and beast, who and what isn't protective of you, Jenna?"

Two dogs sitting at attention in their crates, I gave them a treat and closed their doors.

"Jacob, what do you mean by that snide comment?"

"Nothing, Jenna, thanks for putting the dogs up. I'm sorry, I've just wanted you for so long and first it's the old boyfriend at the airport, and now I'm fighting for your affections against the dogs. I just want you all to myself and I'm not strong in the patience area."

"I'm sorry, Jacob. I want you too. So now you have me all to yourself, what are you going to do with me?"

"Come here!"

"It will be my pleasure, Jacob, I'm sure. I must say if you do anything as good as you kiss, I may die in my sleep tonight. I'll die with a smile, but I'm serious, you are the best kisser I've ever kissed."

"Jenna, do you have a heart condition?"

"Actually, I do. I have a terminal case of, Jacob Jamison."

"Oh… you're asking for it now."

"You're just figuring that out, are you?"

"Oh yeah, you asked for it, baby, here I come."

"Stop, stop, stop I forgot, I have a rule. I don't sleep with a guy on our first date. I didn't even get a movie, just dinner. Man, I must be really desperate."

Jacob immediately scooted to the edge of the bed, shook his head and said, "My Jenna, and her rules." He ran his hand through his hair and was getting off the bed. "Where do you want to go? I'll take you there. Whatever you want to do, we will do it. But know this, Miss Jenna, we will be intimate sooner than later."

"I'm counting on that."

"What are we doing and where are we going, what's the plan?"

"Jacob, I'm a woman and women have the prerogative to change their minds, right? I've decided there is nowhere else I'd rather be than right here, right now, with you, just you and me. I don't care about all the things that a traditional relationship would want and need. All that would be nice, but we've been non-traditional from the first butt-grabbing, tree-swinging first kiss, so why change our winning formula now? I followed all the rules with my first husband, and that didn't work out so well for me, so maybe breaking a few of my own rules won't be a bad thing after all."

Jacob jumped back onto the bed and the kissing took place at once. I think he was afraid I'd change my mind again and didn't want to give me a chance to talk again for a considerable amount of time.

"These sheets are amazing. So are you, but they are so soft and smell amazing!"

"That's my new sheets. I put my personal touch on them when I rinsed them in lavender and lemon water. Ever since I went to Sequim, Washington and experienced the beauty and fragrance of lavender fields, I'm in love with fresh lavender forever. I have them send me fresh lavender products every other month."

"So, to get to your heart, I need to be wearing lavender?"

"Or nothing at all, Jacob…now, where were we? I think you were kissing my neck and doing an amazing job, I must say."

The kissing resumed with fervor and passion, strength and gentleness. Jacob took my body like it had never been touched before. He made sure I had no space unexplored and I was beyond life as I had ever known it. I had goose bumps on top of goose bumps. I had shivers and jerk responses I didn't even know were possible. Words haven't even been invented yet to describe my utter delight and amazement of the passion we launched in each other.

I'd been married but never felt the love and passion I felt right now, right here, with my Jacob. His hairy chest wasn't overpowering, it was just enough with a small line of hair leading down his well-defined abs ending with a line of dark hair leading to his central powerhouse. He has the size and stamina to please a woman every time. I love him. I feel more alive than I've ever been before. I actually have parts alive on me I didn't even know I had. I'm in a mind-numbing sexual high. Heaven… thank you God! Thank you, Jacob. Should I thank him out loud? No Jenna, just breathe!

I've been so consumed with my sexual mind-blowing pleasures that I forgot about trying to please him. I'm sure he's been with many, many women. I've only been with one man, my ex-husband, and our sex life was practically non-existent. Is Jacob satisfied with me? Am I enough to please him? Jacob was breathing heavy, lying next to me with a twinkle in his beautiful blue eyes and a peaceful grin on his handsome face. Then he exhaled my name "Jenna", and showed his full-on beautiful white-teeth smile.

"Yes, my Jacob?"

"You are over the top amazing! Even better than I imagined, and, baby, I have a great imagination."

"Really, Jacob? "You know I don't do lies, a deal breaker, remember? I want you to be happy, I want to please you and if there is anything you want, tell me, it's yours."

"I love you. I told you I loved you before we had sex. But after what we just shared, I'll never love anyone but you. Only you, Jenna. Marry me!"

"Jacob, I love you too, but we can't get married, you don't know me. You really don't know what you're getting into with me. I'm not that exciting. I'm not one of those stylish women that are up to date in the fashion world, compared to you who looks like you just stepped out of a GQ magazine. I'm one of those girls that adores cuddling on the couch and watching movies with popcorn. I love to go to football games, read books, travel to different places, take pictures of nature, and go for walks with my dogs. Or just sit by the fire and roast marshmallows. Jacob, I don't want you to be bored with me after a month or two. I love you and want to be with you, like this, forever. But I couldn't take it if you weren't happy, especially if you weren't happy with me. It would destroy me. I love you too much to not be enough for you."

"Jenna…"

"No, let me finish, Jacob. I was married before. I tried to make it work. Really, I did. But when he found out we couldn't have children then that was the end of our sex life. And that was at the beginning of our marriage. Then Tom got back pain and hooked on prescription drugs and then our marriage spiraled downward quickly. We tried marriage counseling, more than once but it didn't work. I got tired of living with someone who had no idea who I was or what I needed. I would try to talk to him, but he never heard what I said."

"I don't understand. What do you mean by that?"

"Well the first example that comes to mind was our honeymoon. Tom and I planned to go to Hawaii but he had a health issue arise a couple of months before our wedding so we couldn't afford to go on our dream honeymoon and pay hospital bills too. We decided to go to St. Louis for our get away.

He told me our first night together would be at a Best Western in a little town called Belleville, Illinois. I told him no way! I've driven through that town my whole life on my way to Granny and Partner's house and that is not the town that I want to give away my virginity. I gave him options like how about St. Louis? That's a bigger city, with four-star hotels, let's stay there. Or how about we go to Kansas City to celebrate our first intimate night together? That would be a fun town to explore. How about we go to a really nice hotel there? I'm not going to Belleville. Nothing against the town personally, it's just not special in my mind, I don't want that for us on our first night. So, you would think that after this sincere plea, more than once I might add, he would heed my begging and want to please his wife, especially on their honeymoon.

"I honestly thought he was just kidding me to get me going about the location. But no, our honeymoon, Belleville, Illinois, on Main Street, cheap room, not even a honeymoon suite. This hotel didn't have one. Oh, and it gets better, my Granny and Partner actually drove by the hotel on their way home from my wedding and left us a note on our car windshield. True story, I couldn't make this stuff up. I was his wife, we had sex, but my heart was broken that he didn't care about what I said or what I wanted when I'd told him over and over as clearly as was humanly possible. This is not what I wanted. And that was how the rest of our unhappily ever after union continued until I finally left him."

"Jenna, I'm so sorry. He was a moron wrapped up in an idiot to treat you like a generic brand of paper plates, when you are clearly fine china. Baby I love you and I will never treat you like that. I will listen and hear you Jenna. Don't hold Tom's shortcomings against me, against us. We love each other, and I want you forever. I'm not going to be bored with you Jenna. You might be bored with me."

"I live out in the middle of miles and miles of open fields with fences and horses. I run my own businesses, usually from the office but sometimes from home on my computer, and some travel is required. I have an office in a nearby town to keep things and people accountable because my business is constantly growing."

"My Grandmother, as you know, is a powerful woman and has a great deal of money. She has lots of political friends all over the place and tries to be involved in my life on a frequent basis. I don't take money from Grams because I don't want the transfer of ownership of my life to her. I make decent money, so you could be a stay-at-home wife, or work if you want. I'm tight with my money, but if you want to travel and see the world, baby, I want to be there with you. We will make that happen. Your dreams will be mine. I haven't ever been married, but I get that it takes giving and taking on both sides. I have lots of married friends and they all seem to be happy. Marriage can work. I love you, Jenna, and I know you love me, so let's do it baby, marry me. I want to spend my forever with only you."

"I heard what you said, Jacob, and I think we should go shopping."

"What does shopping have to do with love?"

"Ring shopping, I'm going to need a ring, to show the world that I'm yours and you're mine. I love you too, Jacob, I will gladly marry you! If you want forever with me, I want forever with you too."

The kissing resumed, and then the proposal and

acceptance was sealed with round two of our love making marathon session. I don't know if my body can handle a lifetime of him. He's exhausting and exhilarating all at the same time. Our third time was just as exciting as the first two times. I love him, I adore him, I need him, I want him. Will it always be like this? I don't know, but I'm getting married. I've never been happier... *ever!*

Chapter 17

The Engagement

It was so hard to get out of bed and go to work when Jacob was at my house, just waiting for me. I told the girls at work on our lunch break, that I am getting married. I am so excited it sort of jumped out of my mouth without warning. I never planned to tell them, especially before I even told my own family and best friends. They just eyed each other across the table and smiled but no best wishes, nothing. A silent tension filled the air.

The first thing finally announced after I made my exciting announcement is, "Jenna, don't you think you should at least date someone before you marry him?"

"Yes, I know it's all happened suddenly, but we've dated, and we are getting married."

"Just because you sleep with a man doesn't mean you have to marry him, this is the 21st century."

"What's your wedding date? Where are you going for your honeymoon?"

"Let's see your ring!"

Great, all the questions, I'm not prepared, I should have kept my mouth shut! I should have known my co-workers would want details. What should be a joyful announcement is turned into an interrogation.

"Well, we don't exactly have the date set yet, don't know about the honeymoon yet, and we are going shopping for rings in our near future."

I wanted to say thanks girls for all the good wishes, but they didn't wish me well, and I should have known better than to throw this out there without being prepared. I don't think they believe that Jacob even exists. The way they behave will not dictate me sharing my life out loud. I'm excited and even if they aren't happy for me, I am going to share my excitement with anyone and everyone who will listen.

I'm getting married to a beautiful, handsome and loving man. He's the man of my dreams. I have a best friend forever. I'm really excited for my future.

I couldn't wait to get home, to my loving fiancé Jacob. He drove me to work and was going to pick me up after work so we could go to town and find a ring. I thought I could tell the girls he was picking me up, but I didn't need to prove anything to my nonbelievers. I know the truth, and they can choose to believe me or not, it's nothing on me. I'm keeping my Jacob all to myself.

My thoughts jumped to my brother Jeff. I need to tell him and mom about my engagement news soon, maybe tonight. Jeff will blow a gasket when I tell him I've chosen Jacob. I haven't told my family and Jacob hasn't told his. We have so many conversations to have tonight, Jacob my fiancé and me. I'm getting married. I've never been happier with anyone. It sort of feels like a dream and I really hope I don't wake up because my life is never this good in real life. It really feels like I must be dreaming. But better than any dream I've ever had because he's 100% real.

Finally, the end of my school day, I called Jacob to come pick me up from work.

"I'm already parked in the school parking lot waiting on you to get off work. Babe, can I come inside and see your classroom, see where you do your work?"

"Yes of course, I'll meet you at the front door and show you off to those that are still in the building. You're the best show and tell I've ever had Jacob."

"You are a charmer Ms. Jenna. I'm on my way inside now."

He had his cowboy boots on, of course, and his blue jeans, a button down burgundy red shirt and his million-dollar smile. I met him at the door and introduced Jacob to my school secretary, my friend Ms. Becky the real power of any school. She is a sweetie and was one of my friends who helped feed my dogs when I was falling in love with Jacob. Ms. Becky is kind and welcoming as usual.

Then we walked down the hallway to my classroom. As we were entering my room, I heard the teachers on my team leaving for the day. They are close to passing my room. Should I or shouldn't I, that is the question? Oh why not, I want to see their faces, so I stepped into the hall and announced, "Ladies, if you have a minute, I'd like to introduce you to my future husband Jacob."

One teacher said, "I'd like to, but I have to tutor after school and kept walking."

A minute, really can't spare one-minute? The other three teachers walked on saying they were sorry but have after school plans.

"That's fine he's in my room if you want to meet him."

One of the teachers came to my room. She is a sweet young teacher and a friend on the team. She took two steps over to enter my room and introductions were made. She too had to tutor a student after school, so she quickly left.

Jacob is his handsome charming self. I love him. Then we left my room and walked down the hall, hand in hand

and I gave him the whole school tour. He was impressed that a Kindergarten through Fourth grade school had a student body of over 550 students and five kindergarten teachers with 25 students each. This was much larger than the country schools in his local area. I teach at the biggest elementary school in the largest school district in Missouri.

I am thinking to myself, I have worked all day, and tonight we are going looking for rings. Can we get out of here already?

"Will you miss all of this if you can't find a teaching job right away in Kentucky?"

"I will miss my kids, and most of my co-workers that are good friends, but I can keep in touch with a thing called the internet. But I have my principal's degree too, so I could be a principal or teacher and I'd be happy contributing to society in either capacity."

"Well aren't you just full of surprises?"

"On occasion, just wait you'll see."

"Don't do that to me. I've thought about you all day, in your house. All around me the looks and smells of you, and I missed you."

"What did you do today darling?"

"I worked from home honey, on a thing called the internet."

"Touché! Are you hungry? Oh no, I've seen that look in your eyes before, I mean hungry, for food not what you have in mind, well not until later anyway. And are we still ring shopping tonight? What do you want to do my handsome Jacob?"

"I looked on-line at local jewelry stores and read reviews and saw a couple of rings I'd like to see on your hand."

"You are so thoughtful, you are thinking about me, about us today? I love you Jacob!"

"I love you too, my beautiful Jenna."

"What's a girl got to do around here to get a kiss from

the man she loves?"

"I am trying to respect your professional image, at your place of business, but if you don't care, get over here I'll kiss you right here and right now!"

"No, you are right, professional, work. I have a solution to this problem, let's get out of here, it's Friday!"

"After you my little Kindergarten teacher."

Holding hands, we walked back down to my classroom and I got my purse, locked the door and headed out to my car. Jacob opened my car door, buckled my seat belt and kissed me with such affection I am really glad he snapped my seat belt on first or my now limp body would have slid out of my seat and onto the ground in a puddle of goo.

What this man does to me, I'm going to have to step up my game, so he gets a taste of his own medicine. I don't know exactly how to do that, but I need to do something. Who needs to exercise when Jacob raises my heart rate at just a look, but with a kiss it's like a 5-K run, and I've never run a race in my life. But Jacob truly makes my heart not just beat but sing. I'm so happy!

"Shopping then food then it's us time. Hey Jacob, are those my clothes hanging and my suitcase in the back seat?"

"Yes, my observant fiancé, I've packed a few of your personal items for our weekend together."

"Where are we going?"

"We have the weekend at the Hilton reserved downtown Branson, the honeymoon suite to be exact. I want you to have everything you deserve, nothing but the best. I'm so sorry your ex stuck you in a roach motel. We will have room service and sex 24/7 this weekend. Whatever your heart desires, that's what I want to give you."

"Forget the shopping then, let's go to Branson now! Wait Jacob, what about my dogs. I'll need to make arrangements for Molly and Moose."

"I called your friend Sherry and she's going to feed the

dogs while we are on our weekend hiatus. She knows who I am and said she'd be glad to take Molly and Moose for the weekend. She has a key to your house, so I locked the door and headed over here to pick you up."

"How did you know who she is and how to get connected with her?"

"You had her number on the side of your refrigerator under in case of emergency. I thought that this is possibly a mild emergency, so I visited with your friend. I like her, she's really funny."

"Well, it looks like you worked hard today too. Thanks for thinking of us and making arrangements for us to have a special weekend together."

"Sherry didn't seem very surprised when I called her. She said you'd been talking about me non-stop ever since you got back from Kentucky. And that you only had good things to say about me. She wants to meet me to see if I'm really as good looking as you claim."

"Oh she did, did she?" I'll need to have a long conversation with her after Jacob leaves.

"Yes, and she also mentioned she's never seen you so excited and alive and she hoped that I make you this happy forever. Then she informed me that she's older and wiser and if I treat you wrong, she's not afraid to call your cousins and brother and send them to my door. She seemed really charming, your friend Sherry."

"Yes, that sounds like my good friend. Just wait till you get to know her Jacob. She has been a great friend and we've had a great time going to concerts, playing cards, going out and doing craft projects together. She's helped me survive with humor. I want you to take some time to get to know my friends here and to get to know my mom too in the not too far off future.

I know your mom wasn't in the picture for you when you were growing up, but my mom has enough love she can help fill the mom void you've missed out on for many years. She is the most amazing woman I've ever known. She's gone through hardships neither of us will ever face, and she came through them all with her sanity and sense of humor. I adore my best friend, my mom. She knows me better than anyone, and that is probably why I don't think she will be shocked at our wedding news. She has always been there for me and supported me during my cancer, divorce, anything and everything I've been through she's been there with me and for me. I'm sure she will come around to the picture of us when she sees how happy we are together."

"Wait a minute, did you say cancer?"

Chapter 18

The Cancer Discussion

Jacob swerved on the road staring at me. "Yes, but no worries, I'm fine, cancer free and that talk will be for another day."

"No, that talk will be for today and now."

"Why? Are you worried you are handling damaged goods?"

"Jenna, never kid like that, not about your well-being. Cancer is not funny, not ever!"

"Okay, I'll tell you everything, I'm sorry to be glib about such a terrible thing as cancer. I don't think it's funny at all, I just don't think we should be in the car traveling at 70 miles an hour when we have this discussion."

"Well good timing, because right off this exit is the top-rated jewelry store in the Ozarks. I know this because that's what all their advertising says on the internet."

"Oh honey, I've heard about this place and they are really high priced here. Jacob, maybe we should look somewhere else first?"

"Jenna, never skip on quality, it's pricey up front but you can't go wrong with quality. You are quality and you don't have to settle for something beneath you again. I want the best for you Jenna. No pressure with picking out a ring tonight. I want you to have the ring that you will love till we are finally laid to rest. We are forever and your ring needs to be a forever ring too."

I hate seat belts I need to get to Jacob right now. He needs to be kissed and kissed often by me and only me.

"Ring time baby let's go inside. And I need to hydrate your kisses zap me to the core."

"Good." As Jacob walked over to my side of the car to open my door, like a gentleman, I said, "Jacob, just so you know, I've been holding back, didn't think you could handle all of me at once." *I am totally kidding him.*

"Oh no you haven't sweetheart!"

Jacob grabbed me, pinned me up against the side of the car and kissed me like I'd never see him ever again.

"Jacob, (panting breathy) I can't feel my legs. You need to help me walk inside. And okay I lied, I wasn't holding back, but you were holding out on me! I cannot wait for our weekend together. We are going to have the best weekend of my life!"

"Bring it on, my little cast wearing, competitive sweetheart. You are so beautiful Jenna, have I told you that lately?"

"No, as a matter of fact I don't think you've ever told me that. I'm pretty sure I'd remember the man I love saying that to me because it means more than anything coming from you. Clearly, we need to stop and get you an eye exam, but let's wait until after our naked weekend together before we get your glasses."

"Cute and funny, now let's get in there and find your ring."

We looked at rings, and wow they are really expensive. I

am so glad I had a manicure before he came, because my tan hands looked so good with these high-priced rings. I look good in expensive. We found a ring I really like with baguette diamonds around the front of the band and a large sort of octagon center stone, but Jacob wants to surprise me with one of three we liked best. Any three of them are beautiful clarity, cut and a total of three carat diamonds. There might have been some other word that started with a "c" but I don't remember what it was. Jacob apparently knows about diamonds because he knew what to ask and what he wanted. I would be proud to wear any ring Jacob chose for me. He just wanted a plain band for himself. I am having it engraved on the inside of the ring, "Jacob, all my love forever."

Planning on spending lots of money made both of us very hungry. We headed to Branson, the excitement building in my stomach. *What a great way to start our weekend together, with wedding ring shopping. I'm so mad at myself for mentioning that I had cancer. I don't want to waste one more minute with that word, much less reliving the whole nightmare with Jacob. Our time is so short together, I don't want to do the cancer talk, not now, not ever really. Why did I open my big mouth? Maybe he'll forget about it if I do a good job of distracting him. It might be possible I think I am up for this challenge.*

We walked around the riverfront called Branson Landing, watched the outside water and fire show. Listened to live music playing in the piano bar and walked and shopped at different shops along the waterfront area. We watched ducks swim by the shoreline, along with boats and geese as we sat outside on the deck at Joe's Crab Shack and ate fresh catfish looking out over Taney Como Lake. There in the distance stands the Hilton hotel taller than surrounding buildings just taunting me.

"Babe, you want to shop at any of these shops while we are here, they'll be closing soon? Anything in particular you want or need?"

"No, I have everything I need right here just holding your hand. What about you? Is there anything you want to put on a shopping list?"

"No, if you're tired of walking around we could go get settled in at the Hotel, maybe get in the hot tub? Might be fun if we can keep your cast out of the water, we can do it."

"Um, did you pack my suit?"

"Um, you won't need one. I don't want you to think I've tabled this cancer discussion. I want to hear about this when we get to the room and then we can relax and enjoy ourselves."

"Okay Jacob, but I may need chocolates for a discussion of this magnitude."

"That will be fine. I just so happen to see a chocolate shop two stores down from here, so let's hit it and then we can go to the hotel. With milk, dark and white chocolates, the good quality stuff in a large bag, caramels and toffees too, yum yum. We are in the car headed to the hotel. Checked in and up to the top floor, honeymoon suite. This suite had to cost a small fortune, but it is awesome! I wish I had my camera, I'd be taking pictures of this room.

"Jacob, we cannot afford this for the entire weekend. Let's enjoy our time together tonight, but honey this is extravagant, and I don't think we can afford it."

"Sweetheart, don't worry about finances. I've got us covered. That reminds me, I need your social security number for my attorney to put you on my beneficiary paperwork."

"Wait, you already told your attorney we are engaged?"

"Yes, I talked to him on a business matter before I left Kentucky and told him my plans with you and told him to get the paperwork in order."

"Wow, I don't know what to think or say on that, but Jacob, I honestly don't think you get my financial situation. Let me just put all the cards on the table since you are going to be my husband and find this out my financial status soon anyway.

I'm a teacher that didn't start teaching right out of college. I was married at the time and with my husband's paycheck and with what I would be making as a teacher I didn't see a problem for my future. I chose the teaching profession for the love of kids, not for the pay. But I've always had to be very cautious with spending because I have one source of income. It scares me to spend so much money. I appreciate nice things it's just not something I'm used to doing for myself.

"It's a beautiful room and I love that you picked the best for us; I love it I really do. I will appreciate this room and want to enjoy it to its fullest potential with you tonight, but I want you to be able to afford to fly and see me again in the near future, and for me to fly out to see you. I'd rather be with you, spend time together so I can live without the fancy nice things if it gives me more one-on-one time with you. I appreciate you more than words can say Jacob. The fact that you heard me when I told you about my past with Tom, and remembered it and made plans to make me feel special, thank you for hearing me and loving me. I respect your efforts on our behalf. Thank you for this best of the best view of a room. I wish I could buy you the best of the best stuff too, but that's not in my abilities right now."

"No, you won't have to do without, ever again, not as long as I have anything to do with it. I'll show you my business books, checkbook, whatever you want to see. I have full disclosure with you too. My finances are yours. One of my businesses was in Forbes Magazine last year as one of the top 25 small businesses in America. I do very well for myself. I just don't advertise my assets in a public way. I didn't have a choice about the magazine article, it was going to be published whether I gave an interview or not, so I went ahead with the magazine article so I could have my spin on the story. I actually dated the interviewer after the publication for a few months.

I have diverse investments and before I leave Missouri, we are buying you a new SUV. Jenna you cannot drive this stick shift with a cast on your foot. I don't know how you've done it so far, but it's not safe and we are doing the car thing tomorrow. I've already made some calls and we have an appointment tomorrow at 11:00."

"Jacob, I'm really glad you have financial security. It's a big relief to me on one hand and on the other hand it makes me feel like I'm going to freak out! Seriously, why hasn't someone married you before me? You are the hottest man I've ever met in person, smart, caring, funny and rich. Something has got to be seriously wrong with you that I don't know about, because you are too good to be true.

I know no one is perfect, but you are Jacob, and perfect won't fit with me. I'm one of those people that always means well but things usually take many twists and turns before they turn out okay if they turn out okay at all. I'm a neat freak and I like things clean and organized. What are you thinking right now Jacob, are you worried because I'm worried? I'm rambling, I can't figure you out. Jacob, I could never be perfect even if I was trying to do it for you, I am not. What are we going to do?"

"Calm down babe. I'm not perfect, no one is perfect, so don't get stuck on false perceptions. It just took me a long time to find you that's all. We are a good fit, in every position, wink, wink. I love you more than I love myself. That in itself is shocking to me to say that out loud, but it's the truth. I could never be happy if you aren't happy. So, baby you are stuck with me. Rings, wedding, forever that's us Jenna, get used to us because it's going to be our future. I have millions and now you have access to it too."

"Jacob, this is scary for me to ask you, so please don't ask me why I'm asking this now but here goes: do you think you would or could be controlling of me once we get married? Are you the type of man who wouldn't trust me? I need to know that you trust me completely so I can trust you.

Trust and honesty go hand in hand for me. I need someone who trusts me and who isn't going to sneak around and check my emails, phone messages, mail, follow me where I go, check with my friends behind my back. Are you secure enough that you can be secure with me? Are you going to become controlling with me? Do you think you might be with me in the future? I need you to search deep in your soul and tell me the God's honest truth because this is imperative to me."

He just stared at me for what seemed forever but must have only been a full minute, I wondered if he heard me and if this was going to be a problem, I was getting nervous that he was angry I would ask such a terrible thing. I was just about to break the uneasy silence but he finally spoke.

"I want to go and beat Tom's ass. Baby I love and trust you. I am not going to get into your purse unless you ask me to. I'm not checking your phone, messages, mail or any of that crap. I don't want to control you. I want to love you and enjoy you.

You are an amazing woman and I look forward to being with you every moment of our future together. We don't have to get you a car unless you want to, I just really want you to be safe and you need a car made in this decade. But I don't want you to see this as me controlling you because that is not what it is. I love you and when I do things for you it's because I love you not that I'm using my money to control you or manipulate you. I will try to consider what you just told me, so you don't ever feel that way with me. I only want to love, protect and take care of you, you can trust me babe."

"Thank you for being sensitive to my wants and needs, you have no idea how much that means to me and I love you for being you. I do need a new car, and since I know

now that you have money and aren't sacrificing beyond your means for me, I would love to take you up on the car offer. It is very difficult for me to drive a stick shift with a cast on up to my knee. I have worried about safety to be honest with you and I need new tires too, so the timing would be helpful for me.

I love that you think about me and put my needs before yours. I don't even have to say or ask for anything before you are already taking care of things for my best. You amaze me, Jacob you give me so much.

I feel like you are getting the short end of the stick with me. But I love you and will spend my life trying to deserve you. I love you more than I have loved anyone or anything in my life before you. Honestly it scares me how much I totally love you."

"Jenna, don't be so adorable we are having the cancer talk before we have sex tonight."

"I know but it's just this room is so fabulous, and you are off the charts hot. I think I'm going to take a hot shower first. Do you want to join me or wait to chat until after my shower?"

"You don't play fair."

"All is fair in love and war, right? We are in love and oops, there goes my shoe, hey can you help me shimmy out of these tight jeans? Can you help me with this bra, it hooks in the back? What are you doing?"

"I know when I'm beat, but what a way to go. Shower time baby. Am I carrying you or are you walking?"

"Neither, I'm racing you there but with a cast I need a head start."

"Cute, but with your record of running into walls, and since you already have one broken foot, how about I get you there safe and sound?"

I have the trash bag and rubber band to cover my cast, it's such a pain to deal with I can't wait to get this cast off!

That was the best shower I've ever had! He likes the

water hot like I do. The steam filled the room and with 3 pulsating shower heads at different positions on different shower walls, it all just enhanced our shower bliss. So much stimulation, we both came out of there barely able to walk. We literally wobbled to the bed and dropped naked on the comforter. It took several minutes before either of us are able to move.

The bed is premium comfort, you just sink into it like a feather bed without the feathers. Jacob got up grabbed my night shirt and my brush and said, "I'll brush your hair, you talk." He threw on his boxers and brought me a Diet Dr. Pepper out of the stocked fridge and he had his coke. His drink of choice is Jack and coke, but I don't believe he has any kind of a drinking problem. He had done his homework, because the fridge had everything we needed. We took a couple pieces of chocolate from our specialty store, sodas in hand and moved to the television room to talk about my cancer.

Clearly he isn't going to let me off the hook on the topic, so I am going to have to spend our precious time together talking about my past. I don't want him to feel like I'm hiding anything from him or keeping my past from him, so I just need to have this conversation and get it over with. He has a right to know about my health issue to be sure he still wants me in his future. "Jacob, I need to dry my hair really quick then you can brush all you want."

"Babe, here's a chair. You sit in the bathroom on this chair and I'll brush and dry your hair and you relax. I've never done this before, but your hair is so beautiful I just want to do this. Then you can tell me your story and I will listen."

"Jacob, I've never told anyone my cancer story before, so here goes. About 12 years ago, I was living in Wisconsin and married to Tom at that time. I went to my bi-yearly dentist appointment for a routine tooth cleaning and he felt my neck and told me I had a lump that needed to be looked at by my doctor. I took his advice, made an appointment and went to see my doctor. When I got in to see my doctor, she told me it was probably allergies and not to worry about it.

Six months later, when I went back for my dental tooth cleaning again, my dentist said "Jenna, I told you to go see your doctor about that lump." I told him I did and she said it was just allergies. He moved his chair closer to me so I could see his concern and he said, 'You need to find another doctor.' Now worried, I called my regular doctor and asked for a referral to a nose, ears, and throat specialist to check out this lump. She approved it and so the testing began. The tests, retest, ultrasounds, biopsies, needle-guided biopsies etc. Finally, the results were conclusive, and I had thyroid cancer, thus the beautiful scars on my neck."

"Baby I didn't even notice the scars."

"Well, you are either blinded by love or my earlier concern, you need glasses. My first surgery they found the cancer had spread to my lymph nodes." I looked at Jacob and he was tearing up. "Baby, I'm okay it's okay really. After the surgery they had me do heavy duty radiation treatments. My doctor didn't want me to do chemo unless it was the last resort. After surgery and treatments, I still had cancer. Once again, I had to face another surgery. Then once again the results said cancer. I honestly never cried a tear with fear of dying or anything like that."

"My teacher friends in Wisconsin were really my close family and my principal was a sweetheart too. They all poured out the love and they helped me with grocery deliveries, food delivered, etc. They knew my husband wasn't much help, so they stepped in and saved me during that difficult time. My principal even called Tom into his office to give him a man to man talk of how he needed to take care of me now. I was shocked he did that, but eternally grateful for a Christian man who could see my need and step up and do what he could to try to help me and Tom!"

"Well the third time they told me I had to be cut open because I still had cancer, my dad said enough was enough. Dad insisted he'd pay the difference of what my insurance wouldn't cover if I would go out of my insurance plan and get to Mayo Clinic for a second opinion and a solution. My local doctor that I really loved and respected sent a letter on my behalf to Mayo Clinic requesting that they invite me to be their patient. I was invited to be a patient and my third surgery was at Mayo Clinic in Rochester MN. This place is like a city unto itself. They had machines that were the latest fastest things I'd ever been in. All in all, Mayo is a very impressive top of the line medical organization."

"While I'm getting out of the car thinking about what tests I would be having run, Tom is getting out of the car with me to go inside the building and something blew in his eye walking me into the hospital. He left me on our first visit there, in an office by myself and he took off to find an eye specialist to help him with his eye.

I think his bill for services cost more than mine did that day. I had no idea where he was, and I just had to wait until he eventually showed up long after all my tests were taken and completed. He didn't meet any of my doctors and wasn't there for me. I sat there worrying about him the whole time. I had to go through all that by myself. That was Tom. He always meant well but in reality he was never there for me."

"Mayo doctors assured me that they would get it all, and that I wouldn't have to do any more surgeries after they took care of me. They were a professional team and knew their stuff. I was very impressed and they scheduled my surgery. My mom drove 13 hours non-stop to get there for me to take me to Mayo.

Tom stayed home because he wasn't feeling well, and he really was more work than help, so I could just relax and know my mom would take care of me. The surgery went well, they got it all; and I've been clean for my five-year danger zone check-ups, so it's all good now. I no longer have a thyroid, or a lot of lymph nodes. I have to take an artificial thyroid pill each day, but other than that, I'm healthy and drug free. Just have these three scars on my neck from the three different surgeries."

"I only took one Tylenol for a pain reliever after my third and last surgery because God was with me and I really had no pain through the whole process. God is with me and my family, mom, dad, brother and sister-in-law were all there for me every step of the way. I look back at that time, and I honestly thought my cancer was a gift to let me see how much I was loved by others. I thought that cancer was going to be my ticket out of my marriage."

I thought I would just die and not have to go through a divorce. I didn't believe in giving up and a divorce was a public announcement that I was a failure. I thought this was my way out of this life sentence of a marriage and I was fine with whatever God had planned. But I didn't lose my life, God spared my life . I try each day to be a blessing and count my blessings."

"Jacob, you are an unexpected blessing, and the joy of my heart. I don't want to sound over religious, but I do have a personal relationship with God. I believe the Bible is true and I know He's helped me when I couldn't help myself."

Jacob was sympathetic during my entire discussion and didn't say a word, he just pulled me to his side and carried me back to the bed. Just before I fell asleep, I heard him tenderly whisper, "I'm so glad you are okay, because I love you so much Jenna." I just squeezed him tighter and we fell asleep in each other's arms. So much for sex and the hot tub plan, but it was so wonderful to have his strong arms wrapped around me. His heat next to me and his strong steady breathing relaxed me.

Chapter 19

Our Baby

We slept the entire night. 7:00 a.m. and we both moved out of each other's arms and were wide awake. Jacob wanted to hit the gym downstairs. I'm not a workout sort of girl but didn't want him going down, seeing hot girls, exercising all by himself, so I went too. Shockingly Jacob had packed my sweats and tennis shoes. He thinks of everything. I wonder if Sherry helped him because he did a great job being prepared.

After our workout, I did feel more energetic. It's hard to work out with a cast on your foot, but I just rode a stationary bike while I watched him do weights and run on the treadmill. Then we went upstairs and here we are again in this amazing shower. No need to re-tell what went on there. But we didn't stay in the shower as long this time. We got out and dressed, ready for our car shopping day ahead.

We ate breakfast on the Branson strip, at a mom and pop

home cooking restaurant. Thank goodness we worked out, because with yummy homemade buttermilk biscuits, country gravy, ham, eggs, pancakes, and coffee, we were stuffed. And the best freshly squeezed orange juice, yummy. The Ozarks and homemade food, so down home good, it's bad.

Jacob was quiet and I just wanted to hear his voice. "You're so quiet this morning, what are you thinking about? Did my cancer past freak you out last night? It's not too late to back out of forever with me."

"No, I'm sorry, babe. I've been a little distracted because I got an email on my phone this morning when you were drying your hair. My ranch manager informed me my favorite horse, Chief, ran through a barbed wire fence last night during a thunder and lightning storm. The vet came out this morning. They had to put him down."

"Oh no, Jacob, I'm so sorry."

"I'm fine, just hate I wasn't there with Chief. He was an amazing, fast running horse. I made a lot of money in stud fees with him because he is from an impressive bloodline and he ran with all his heart. A little on the wild side, he'd spook easy. I should have had all wooden fences up by now, but my farm hands hadn't finished putting up my new fencing because I kept putting them on other projects. I hate that he went out that way. I'll be fine, just sad news. Let's talk about something else."

"I'm so sorry, Jacob. I know if something happened to my dogs, I'd be inconsolable. Let's cancel the car appointment today and just walk around town, maybe go fishing if you would enjoy that. I want to do something you want to do, Jacob."

"Babe, I want to get you a car today. We are trading in your car, unless you want to keep it?"

"Honey, buying a car and a ring that's a lot of money. You're spending a lot of loot for me and I don't want you to think I need your money to be happy, I just want you. I don't want to be a financial drain on you. Or for you to ever question my love has nothing to do with your bank accounts."

"I've told you this won't be a noticeable impact on me at all. So, we are doing this? And fishing? Since when do you like to fish? I don't remember you ever going fishing with us growing up."

"That's because I've never gone fishing with you. I think I've been fishing once or twice in my whole life but not really had a good time. I caught one fish, a perch in Partner's pond once, but it was too small, and I had to unhook it and throw it back. And the fins on the top of the fish were sharp and cut my hand, so not so much fun.

However, I do enjoy riding in boats, and skiing, both snow and water. I just thought you being a man's man, would like fishing, and there are lots of lakes around here. I just want you to have fun. I want you to be happy, Jacob, you are my focus, and I love you and wanted to do something you'd enjoy."

"Babe, I do enjoy fishing, but I haven't fished in years. The last time was with my brothers after my Grandpa passed away. After the funeral, we changed out of our suits and got out on the water and fished for hours. We all caught our limits, had several beers, and that was my last fishing trip."

He hugged her. "I am having fun with you. While at your house, I noticed you have an eye for wall arrangements, and you really are a great amateur photographer. I'd like to help you develop that talent and skill with your photography. Perhaps you can take some photos while we are here."

"Oh, do you like to take pictures?"

"Well I haven't really taken many pictures, but I have a side business that does on-line photo touch ups. I have some connections in the art world too, so I know people who could help us advance your interests and talents. But only if that is something you enjoy and would want to pursue."

"Thanks for noticing my photos at the house. You pay attention to details and I admire and greatly appreciate that characteristic about you. Thanks, and yes, I would love to be a better photographer. I just have a digital camera, so it's not complicated, it's more point, shoot, and hope that I'm lucky. But I really enjoy taking pictures it's exhilarating and relaxing to me.

Jacob, I've been talking about me, me, and me. I want to know you. Are you healthy? Any cancer in your past, any sexual transmitted diseases? What things do you enjoy? What is our life going to be like when we live at your place in Kentucky? Is that what you want for us?"

"I would love for you to live in my, no, in our home in Kentucky if you would like that too. That would make me very happy. You can make any changes at the house you want. We are definitely bringing your new sheets with us because they are as soft as heaven's clouds! We may need to pick up a few more sets of those before I go back. I'm healthy, always have been. I noticed how you sandwiched in the sexual question, and I am clean in all areas, Jenna."

I am sort of a loner, I guess you could say. I like to ride horses to unwind and I also try to see my Grandma at least once a month, usually the last Sunday of each month for family dinners." He paused.

"My mom left me and my dad when I was little. She didn't like my Grandma running my dad's life and my dad didn't like her sleeping around, and I hated them fighting all the time. They divorced.

Dad is the oldest son and when Grandpa was getting older and losing his mental sharpness, he felt Grams needed him in a greater capacity. Grams put dad in charge of a large section of her land and businesses years ago, and over time dad became Grandma's full-time business partner.

I have lots of cousins, and we had a great time growing

up on the farm doing all sorts of things, riding horses, killing snakes, tending cows, building forts, hunting, four wheeling and fishing. I partied pretty heavy in college. My freshman and sophomore years are sort of a blur, but I pulled myself together my junior and senior years. I drink on occasion now, but I haven't been drunk or passed out since my sophomore year, except for a couple times my junior year of college."

"I like my Jack and Coke early evening to take the edge off the day, but if that bothers you, I would give that up as easy as you could give up your Diet Dr. Pepper. It's more of a habit than something I need."

"I have a Dalmatian named Charlie and he runs with me in the mornings. He's an outside dog and has fought coyotes, foxes, muskrats, you name it. He is missing part of his left ear where something ripped it off in a fight. But he is very affectionate and loyal. He rides with me in the truck when I run to town for supplies. I have a few cats that live in the barn and they keep the mice away. I don't have animals in the house, but I would be okay with your Molly and Moose in the house if you want to keep them as house pets."

"Once a week I drive to the nearest town and get things I need for the farm, groceries, and make business connections. But I'm pretty much just on my farm and taking care of business. See, Jenna, country boy and boring."

"And your evenings, what do you do with your evenings, Jacob? You seem to have skipped that part in your description."

"Let me think, if it is harvest time then I'm with all my brothers, cousins, and hired hands in the fields working our own land and Grandma's land too. But if it's not, then basically it's television, reading, computer work, or something to work on or repair on the farm."

"I will admit there are local women who come over for a

'visit' on occasion. I grill them a steak and then we have sex. I do not love any of them and have never told them that I did. That will all change after we are married."

"No, Jacob, that will all change now, this very minute, this very second!"

"I see. I stand corrected. You are so cute, Jenna. Okay, that starts now."

"I shouldn't have interrupted you, sorry I blurted out. You've had multiple partners. Like how many would you say?"

"That's not a healthy direction to go."

"Maybe not for you, but I want to know. I've been with one man and my first time wasn't until my wedding night. And now I'm with you, the man of my dreams. So, there you have it, a grand total of two sexual partners for my entire life. So yeah, I want to know what we are looking at. Ten women, twenty, thirty, hundreds, thousands, don't make me go on. What are we talking about here, Jacob? Do I need to go to a clinic and be tested for sexually transmitted diseases?"

"Babe, I haven't kept track of every encounter and as I told you earlier, college years are sort of a blur."

"How many women were there, Jacob, you aren't in trouble, I just want to know?"

"I'd guesstimate maybe in the 170 to 200's maybe up to 300's category. Could be more or less, but I've never told any of them I loved them. I'm only in love with you. I'm only marrying you."

"Jacob, do you expect me to believe that you never told your fiancé before me that you love her?"

"Well yes, I stand corrected, again. But she's no longer a part of my equation. She's dead. I broke up with her before she died. So yes, I thought I loved her at one time, but she's passed away, and no other living woman besides my mom has heard me say those words.

"Here's the car dealership, babe. We've covered a lot of

topics the last twenty-four hours. Are you up for making a car choice? I should have asked you before now, but do you have a car preference?"

"Honestly, Jacob, I'm afraid I couldn't even afford upkeep and maintenance for this brand. I appreciate your thoughtfulness, but I'd be much more comfortable in an upscale Ford, Chevy, or Toyota SUV. There's a Ford dealership just down the road from here. If that's okay with you since it is your money.

My dad always liked Ford trucks, so I guess that's why I want to try that brand. I haven't read Car and Driver magazines or car reviews, so I am at a loss of what retains resale value, etc. so I'll trust your car expertise. I hate the negotiations for price and payments stuff so if you are up for that then I'm more than ready to get an automatic transmission SUV, so let's do this."

"I'm all over the negotiations. That's what I do for a living, so I'm very comfortable doing this for you. If you promise me to wear your seatbelt, I'll do the rest. Do you want to keep your car, or trade it in?"

"If it will help you pay for my new car, take it. If it won't help, I have a friend that could use a reliable car and I could give it to her. She has three boys and going through a divorce. But I don't know if she'd want a stick shift or not? I'm sure a 1999 Toyota SUV isn't going to have a huge impact on the down payment. Whatever you think, Jacob, I trust you."

"Thanks for the vote of confidence. Your trust means the world to me" He planted a passionate kiss on my lips. "I think you would look good in a candy apple red SUV, am I right?"

"Yes, that would be my first choice. What color interior do you think I want?"

"Hum, black, no… tan leather."

"Wow you are good at this game. What else would I want, Jacob?"

"Sun-roof, like you have now, heated seats, top of the line from wheels to floor mats, nothing but the best for, my Jenna. You ready for a test drive?"

"It sounds like a perfect fit. But Jacob once you smell that new car smell when you take a test drive, you will want a new car. Are you sure, double sure that this won't be an imposition for you financially or any other way?"

"Do you want to see my checkbook? I have money and it's yours, all yours. Jenna, let me do this, it's nothing for me. Besides this will be our car."

"No, Jacob, because if it's 'our' car then what happens to me if you change your mind in a month and don't want to marry me, and want your half of my new car, what do I do then with no car to have for a backup plan?"

"First of all, I will put the new car in your name alone so if for some reason in an alternate universe setting we don't get married, you would have a consolation prize, the new car. Secondly, I am going to marry you and I'm not changing my mind. When are you going to believe me? What do I have to do to prove I love you? Jenna what, tell me?"

"I'm sorry. I love you so much, but you haven't had the past I've had. I guess my baggage is low confidence when it comes to me believing I could be long term loveable. I guess you will have to remind me every day with hugs and kisses that you love me. I want you and need you, Jacob. That's hard for me to admit I need someone and even harder for me to depend on a man to be there for me when I need him. If I say much more, I'll be crying, and I hate to cry. This is just a big decision and I wanted to cover all the bases before we do this. I didn't mean to doubt you."

Jacob came over with a hug and kisses. "I love you, Jenna, you self-doubting adorable fiancé. Now let's go and buy this car, if you like the test drive. Then we can go to the hotel and take a trip to the hot tub. What do you say to that?"

"Sold and hot tub here we come. But my cast will be an obstacle we will have to work around because I'm out of trash bags and rubber bands."

"We can stop at the store and get whatever you need to keep your cast dry. Now let's take that test-drive and see if this is your car, Jenna. There is no pressure, we can look at any dealership you want, so don't think you have to get this car today."

"I love this car, Jacob, it's perfect for me! The smell of this car alone makes me want to pay the $500 plus a month for these wheels of loveliness. What do you think, Jacob? It has good acceleration, cruise control, heated seats, decent gas mileage, and a sunroof. I think it will handle fine in the roaming hills of Kentucky too. What should we name her? She's our baby."

"Okay, then how about Baby?"

"That works for me. Let's take Baby to the hotel!" I was shocked when Jacob told the price he'd pay and charged it on his credit card. I wondered what kind of credit limit allows you to charge $40,000 for a car? When we had keys and a keyless remote in hand, I had to ask. He said he will pay for it in full when he gets his credit card bill, this way he gets frequent flyer points. Was he kidding me or not? I just shook my head.

"Thank you, thank you, thank you, Jacob, I love my new car and love and adore you. Don't you just love the new car smell?"

"Sure, it's great, but not as great as you smell. I like your perfume, and your breath is so sweet. It tastes sweet, and smells sweet, even after your morning coffee. I don't know how you do it, but you are sweet through and through."

"Jacob, I can't wait to get you back to our hotel room to show you how thankful I am for your many kindnesses. I'm thinking our itinerary should include the hot tub, chocolate, sex, chocolate, sex, and then have dinner. Hey tonight do you want to go play putt-putt golf, race go carts, or attend a country western live music show? What do you want to do while we are in the hopping metropolis city of Branson, Missouri?"

"I'm thinking our itinerary should include the hotel, hot tub, sex, chocolate, sex, dinner, and sex. Maybe go to the Titanic museum or the Ripley's Believe it or Not Wax Museum. They have been running ads on my phone. Then back to the hotel and more hot sex. How's that sound to you?"

"I'm with you, your plan sounds wonderful. You always seem prepared, like you've already thought about things before I have even brought them up for discussion. I'm going to have to step up my game with you sweetheart. I'm not used to a man working with me and thinking ahead of me. I love that you work with me and everything isn't a fight against each other. It's so nice to be in love with someone who is on my team. I feel secure and loved, thank you for being you, Jacob. I feel like you've got my back, my front, my sides…anything you want, I'm yours."

"We're good together, a good fit. By the way, we are at the hotel. Should we park Baby in the underground garage or outside?"

"Let's park her inside the garage. We wouldn't want any birds leaving a deposit on our girl. And can I just say I love this new car smell."

"To the top floor, our honeymoon suite awaits. And hash tag, the best, most personally eventful weekend ever!"

Chapter 20

The Wedding

We didn't leave the hotel. Our tentative plans to tour Branson, which is actually a fun town, changed because our personal tour of just the two of us was all consuming. He is so attentive to my needs and wants, my every response is like he can read my mind. I know every woman within a ten thousand-mile-radius of my future home is going to hate me, and with very good reason. Jacob is off the market and he's mine, all mine.

"When do you want to get married? What month and year would be best for your business? When is best for you to get away for a week off to go on our honeymoon?"

"How about we do it tomorrow? We could fly to Vegas unless you want the formal traditional wedding. Girls are into the wedding stuff more so than guys. Whatever you want to do is fine with me, as long as I get the end result and that would be you married to me, making me the luckiest man alive."

"After being with you, I can't imagine not being with you every day of forever. I will marry you in Vegas, tomorrow. But we have to fly my mom along with Jeff and his family for witnesses. I really want my Mom to be by my side. Who do you want for your best man?"

"My best man should be my younger brother Andrew, but he's busy with Grandma's business and wouldn't be able to get off work on such short notice. Since Jeff will be here, and he's going to be my brother anyway, he might as well be my best man."

"No, we can slow this down and wait so you can have your family there with us too. Whatever you want to do, I will wait so we don't hurt anyone's feelings. With my job, we need to see about how I can get out of my teaching contract so that I'm free to move to Kentucky to be with you. You've never been married before. I want to be sensitive to what you want for your only wedding. There won't be any do-overs for you, my handsome hunk of a man."

"You are funny. Babe, my job is on the computer for a majority of my dealings. I can stay with you until we finalize a date for both of our families to join us for our wedding. Would you rather get married on a beach somewhere instead of Vegas?"

"Yes, I would actually love that idea! I don't really want to start our married life off in sin city. Although my honeymoon thoughts for you are borderline sinful. I don't want to "gamble" with our love and our future. I just said yes to Vegas because you mentioned it and I thought that's what you wanted. But a beach would be my first pick. I'd love that if you would."

"We have the location so now we need to pick a date. Let me look at my calendar, it's on my phone. Do you have your calendar? If not, we can set a date a little later. You will need time to shop for your dress, etc. And Jenna I promise you I will listen to you and we will honeymoon in a place that will make up for the pain of your last honeymoon experience."

"Thank you, sweetheart. I trust you to make our honeymoon memorable in a good way, no, in a great way. If I didn't trust you completely, I wouldn't be marrying you, Mr. Jamison!"

"What beaches interest you? How about we go someplace neither of us has been before, a new beginning, an adventure for both of us. We have time to look on the internet to do some research to find our place in the sand. I've been to Hawaii, Kauai, Aruba, St. Thomas, Mayan Rivera, Dominican Republic and that's all I can remember off the top of my head. Jacob what beaches have you been to that would be on your list of already been there and done that?"

"College spring breaks I went to beaches, but I drank heavy back then and the beach wasn't my focus, it was the topless women that caught my eye. Any beach on your wish list is fine with me, babe."

"I've always wanted to go to Australia, but the flight would be way too long for us on a honeymoon. I'd like to go on an African animal picture safari, but again not on our honeymoon. Can you tell I like saying the word honeymoon, honey?"

"Yes dear."

"Get used to saying those two words to me, because you'll be saying them a lot once we are married."

"Yes, dear."

"You're doing fine, keep it up."

"And, Jenna, you'll get used to saying those words to me."

"Ha ha!" Then I immediately jumped back because Jacob tried to swat me on the butt. However, even with a cast on my foot I was able to move quick enough to playfully miss his tease.

"Hey, what do you think about going to Bora Bora,

Bermuda, or Trinidad? I don't know, just envisioning white sand and crystal-clear waters, snorkeling, and rubbing up against your body in the ocean. I can't wait. The more I think about this Jacob, I'm thinking we should wed locally so it won't be so expensive for our families."

"Sweetie, all my family can afford to go wherever you want this shindig to occur. Your brother and sister-in-law make good money too. So that just leaves your mom. I would be glad to cover your mom's expenses so she's not going to have to worry about money. I know your mom is an important person in your life. I will make sure she's here for you."

"I really don't want a big wedding. I did that last time, and it was one big nightmare. I'm not one of those girls who dreamed about her wedding all her life. I seriously wanted to just elope for my first wedding. But the only person I knew who eloped was my uncle Thomas. I called him and his wife and told them of my dilemma and asked them what they would recommend, elopement or big wedding. My aunt said I should have the wedding, that I would regret not having the pictures to share with my kids later in life of my wedding day, the official beginning of the two as one. So, with that advice, I scheduled my big wedding."

"At that time, my mom lived far away, so I only had my dad to help me. My dad's wife made things very difficult for me during the planning of my wedding at every turn. She griped and complained that my wedding dress cost more than hers. I told my dad I didn't go to school dances and spend money on special dresses, or proms, and spend money on all those dresses, but I wanted to buy the dress that made me feel special. And I told him if his wife added up all the money she spent on all five of her ex-wedding dresses, my dress would be a lot less money anyway. My dad and I laughed over that one. He told me not to pay any attention to what she said, he didn't listen to her so there was no reason I needed to worry about what she said either."

"Dad wanted to pay for my wedding, but no money was coming from the step. We both laughed out loud on that one too. My dad bought me the dress I found that made me feel beautiful. I love my dad, but never liked his choice for his third wife, I tried to be nice in spite of her words and actions so it wouldn't cause dad problems to spend time with me."

"There wasn't one thing that went smoothly during the whole pre-wedding and wedding day process. You know, looking back, everything was a battle or fight even up to and including the day of my wedding. Your wedding day is supposed to be the bride's day, but that didn't happen for me."

"Why wasn't your day special for you?"

"I didn't say it wasn't special. But for instance, my two-thousand-dollar wedding dress wouldn't fit the day of the wedding. My beautiful, expensive dress was too big and literally falling off my shoulders. My brother had to go out to his pick-up truck and get fishing line out of his toolbox to sew crisscross across my back to keep my top from falling off down to my waist during the ceremony. See how these kinds of things happen to me. Seriously, I had so many dress fittings, but on the day of my wedding, my top kept falling off. Thank goodness Jeff had his truck and fishing supplies close. I guess you could say Jeff has always had my back."

"Another problem was that my cake had layers and levels with real red roses and bridges with red running water fountains connecting each cake. The day of the wedding, when setting up my cake, it didn't have a groom and bride topper. The cake decorator said I was supposed to supply that. Really, I was going to pay her to do everything but the top of the cake that everyone notices? So, I had another fire to put out on my day. My sister-in-law offered to drive out to her house in the country, get her topper from her wedding cake five years earlier, dust it off, and bring it to put on top of my cake. So that's what we did, I had to have a topper and the cake lady didn't bring extra roses to put on top, so that was the cake."

"Are you ready to run yet? I could give you stories all day long. My ring was another problem. We went to a local jewelry store where my dad bought stuff for my step-monster frequently. They quoted us a price for a ring and wrote it down on their business card. I loved the ring. It was one hundred percent better price than any speck of a diamond we could afford anywhere else. But when Tom and I went back that same afternoon, the owner came out and said he couldn't sell it to us for that amount. I had the card and the price the salesclerk wrote. Because dad was a good customer, he said he would sell it to us at his cost. We paid monthly payments with no interest until paid off, but not for the price quoted in writing."

"Nothing about my first wedding was smooth. I should have never married Tom. I should have taken the heavenly hints and cancelled the wedding. He is a good guy, and we had some good times, but I should have just been his friend and never married him. That's on me. I wanted to be in love. He is smart, funny, handsome, and a nice guy. I just shouldn't have said I do."

"Tom's dad actually told me the night of the rehearsal dinner that it was too late to back out. I was shocked he'd say that to me. I told him not to worry, I loved his son and I was planning on marrying him."

"Someday if you want, I'll show you pictures and I'll give you the play by play and all the other nightmare stories of my first wedding, but only if you want to know all the details."

"I told you all that to say I want to be your wife and let's just elope. I don't need the big wedding. But since you've never had a wedding before, I really want to know what you want? I want you to be happy and have no regrets, not with me, not ever. What are you thinking? I've been talking a lot. Did I share too much about my past?"

"I think you are jumping all over the board with our wedding plans. First let's get married in Vegas, then no to Vegas. Then you want a beach wedding, then a local wedding, then no to a local wedding, then you want to elope, what do you want? How can I get you what you want when you don't even know what you want? It's my job to make you happy. If you are happy, I will be happy."

"Honestly, in the big picture, I just want you, Jacob. The rest is all frosting. You are my main focus and my only desire. If you weren't so handsome, smart, and kind, I would have never had sex before marriage. Seriously, I can't believe I have given myself to you so totally and completely from our first meeting. I am still shocked that I jumped into your arms on our first kiss. I have never done that before to anyone, ever. I don't know how to explain how happy you make me, but it's like my body knew you were my better half before my mind could get used to the idea."

"I love you too. Your heart is so pure, your words are so kind. I'll work from your house this next week, and we will do blood work and get our marriage license ready for when you decide what you want for our wedding. Whenever the paperwork is ready, we can go to the courthouse, church, or beach, and say our 'I do's'. You just need to decide what you really want, then let me know. I'll make it happen."

"I don't know, I can't think clearly when I feel rushed or overwhelmed. All I can think of is how much you get me and love me anyway. I love you so much it is shocking to me. I just want to be with you forever. I feel like I need to marry you quick before you come to your senses and change your mind."

"Not to change the subject or anything, but I've been thinking. My school can get a teacher as a full-time substitute for me the rest of the school year and I could be a substitute in Kentucky until a full-time job becomes available for me to apply. In the meantime, could I help you with your work? I am a pretty fast typist, I can answer phones, and I'm willing to travel."

"I'd be glad to call around and send out some e-mails in my area and see if there are any teaching or principal positions. I'll find out what you need to do to teach in another state. Baby, I'm going to take good care of you and if you don't get work, you will never have to worry about money. But I want you to work at something you find rewarding and challenging. As long as you love teaching, teach. I will support you in whatever you want to do. If you don't have a job, we could travel, you could take pictures. Our possibilities are endless."

"Now it's time to check out of our honeymoon suite, and go back to my place. We have family to call and share our good news. We are in love and going to be married! I'm so happy."

When we got back to my house, Jacob received pictures on his phone of his business. Someone had broken into one of his office buildings. I could see he wanted to go check things out himself. I told him I had to work all next week anyway and I had evening tutoring jobs, so he might as well go back and take care of his business.

It was hard being a grown-up and acting responsible, when all I wanted to do is to be with the man I love and have him stay with me. It was all I could do not to burst into tears telling him to go back to Kentucky without me. I knew he wanted to stay with me, but he wants to take care of his business too.

With our weekend coming to an end, I left for work in my new SUV, and Jacob got a taxi to the airport. Our plan was to be together again in three weeks. This time, I am flying out to him. I'm counting the days already.

We talked on the phone every night and sometimes he'd

call in the morning to wake me up. What a great way to wake up with his strong, low voice saying good-morning beautiful!

I cannot believe I am awake. I have to be dreaming because things are just too good to be true for me. That being said, things didn't stay in the euphoric phase long, because I got a call that changed my everything forever.

Chapter 21

The Murder

"Jenna, darling, I'm sorry to call you at work. I know you're not supposed to take calls on your cell during your workday, but I've got some bad news I need to tell you before you hear it from someone else. Can you talk privately for a minute?"

"Jacob, I only took your call because I saw it was from you. I don't have students right now. My students are at Music and then they go to P.E. class. I have about thirty minutes. You are sort of scaring me, are you alright? What is it, sweetheart?"

"I have terrible news, are you sitting down?"

"I am now, what is it? Tell me you are okay!"

"I'm alright. It's not me, it's Grandma Ruth. She has been shot and pronounced dead at the hospital. Your Grandma was with her. She got beat up something sick and they've rushed her to the hospital too. She's not doing well. She may not make it either."

"Oh my gosh, Jacob, I'm so sorry for Ms. Ruth. Is anyone with my Granny?"

"Yes, the police are questioning her, but she's not doing well enough to communicate with the officers. I have an e-ticket waiting for you at the airport. Pack your bags, pet carriers and dogs, and you and your dogs can stay with me for as long as you want or need."

I got off the phone, immediately went to my principal and told her what happened and explained my need to take a leave of absence. I assured her I will let her know when I know more. I signed the form for leave without pay and left not knowing what I would be facing when I get there, or how I'd pay my bills when I get back home. All I know is I needed to get to my Granny as quick as I can. It's a matter of life and death. She just lost Partner, now she's alone and beat-up. This is outrageous!

I called mom from the car on my way home to pack to tell her about Granny's terrible news. She had already been contacted by the police because she is the oldest child and first on Granny's call list. She is calling her brothers and sister and trying to work out who is going now and what they needed to do. They all had just come home a week earlier. I reassured mom that I would be there for Granny.

I told mom I'd be staying at Jacob's and I'd go to the hospital for Granny until she and her siblings can get there. Poor Granny, she has to be shaken up. What kind of crazy person can kill and beat old women? In that small town, country good ol' boys' area, where everybody knows each other, and they all grew up together. I just can't wrap my head around this. Jacob sounded shaken and that breaks my heart too. I need to be there for him. Poor Ms. Ruth, I can't believe she's gone. She was so strong and healthy and now she's gone. This is mind boggling; I don't understand this at all. I've got to get there as quickly as possible. I need to see my Granny.

Jacob met me at the airport. I don't know how long we

kissed but people were pushing by us and making comments about getting a room and neither one of us cared. There is plenty of room; they could easily get around us with luggage and all. We walked to a special area to pick up my dogs from the flight and my luggage, and we were on the road, buckled up and headed straight to the hospital.

"What have they found out so far? Anything new?"

"Your Grandma has internal bleeding, and she may lose an eye. She got beat over pretty bad, some bones in her face look broken and her ribs are crushed. Her vital signs are really weak. My Grandma was shot in the stomach and bled to death before they could stop her bleeding."

"I'm so sorry, Jacob. How are you and your family dealing with this?"

"My family is preparing for a funeral. We are all worried about your Grandma too. We want answers, so we need to focus on your Grandma. She is in and out of consciousness and is in the intensive care unit now. There is a full-time police officer posted outside her door for protection."

"Protection, what do you mean protection?"

"If her assailants know she's still alive, they may think she can identify them, and she would be a sitting duck in her condition. She has mumbled some things to the police. I have a good friend that's the lead detective on this case, Melissa O'Brian, and she's shared what she knows with me so far. Your Grandma looks really bad; black, blue, and bloody. You need to prepare yourself. She may not even recognize you. Do you want me to go into the hospital room with you? Take your dogs to my place first? What do you want me to do?"

"First of all, thank you for my ticket so I can be here for my Granny. Jacob, you are so kind, so good to me. I've missed you and love you so much."

We are in the hospital parking lot. Seatbelts came flying off and we are going at each other like a couple of high school hormonal kids. I guess it is the stress, the pain of the situation, and the joy of seeing each other, that we just lost ourselves. I don't know how much time had passed when we pulled ourselves off each other, but Jacob is combing through his hair with his fingers and chuckling under his breath while looking in the rearview mirror.

"What's so funny, handsome?"

"You know some parking lots have security cameras. And we just gave the hospital security an 'R' rated show just now."

"Jacob, you'd better be kidding me." I looked up at the parking lot lighting, and sure enough, there were cameras attached to the light poles. In a small town, this is going to be the talk of the town. "Great, you could have told me before I threw myself at you!"

"Ah now what fun would that be? I may find security and order a copy of our parking lot hookup. Who knows, we may already be going viral."

"That is not funny, Jacob, not funny at all. You go get that tape, please, get that tape!"

"Don't worry, those cameras don't work anyway. But if it will make you feel better, I'll check on it before we leave here today."

"Well I think we've done all the damage we can do out here. We should go inside and see Granny. Do you think the dogs will be fine in their kennels if they stay in the back of your pick-up?"

"Sure, they will be fine, just wanted you to have a say. I don't want to be controlling."

"Where'd that come from? I can't believe you just said that to me. Jacob, I'm very emotional with all this right now, as I'm sure you are too. Please don't use personal information I've told you about my past and throw it up in my face during a difficult time. If you need clarification then here it is… I don't see you as controlling, I see you as thoughtful, caring, and helpful. I love you. Now let's go and see my Granny. Hopefully she's feeling better and can answer our questions."

"Are you sure you want to go inside with me? Some people can't handle hospitals. And with just losing your Grandma, I want to be sensitive to your needs too, Jacob. I absolutely hate, no I despise hospitals. The very smell of them almost makes me nauseous. I just lived in and out of hospitals for six years with my dad and his cancer and after my cancer experience, it's almost all I can do to just walk inside one to this day. How mentally irrational is that?"

"I want to be there for you, babe, so of course I'll go inside with you. I didn't realize how difficult this would be for you. I shouldn't have sent you a ticket. I should have just let your mom and her siblings handle all of this. I just wanted to be with you, and I know you and your Granny are really close, being the only granddaughter and all. Sorry, I should have stayed out of this and you wouldn't be here dealing with the stress of this situation now."

"No, sweetheart, you are amazing, I love that you thought of me and helped me to be here for my Granny and my family until everyone can get here. We just buried Partner and I don't know how Granny will deal with this trauma too. Come inside with me Jacob, I want to go see her right now". We walked in the hospital, found ICU, and told we have to put on hair nets, gowns, shoe covers, and gloves. We looked like walking blueberries.

"Jacob, are all of these precautions really necessary? She must be in worse shape than I imagined." I sent up a silent prayer.

"I don't know but hospitals have policies and protocols, and we need to follow them if we want to see your Grandma. We are lucky they are letting us in to see her at all."

There is a police officer sitting in a chair outside of Granny's room. His name tag said Officer Buckle. I felt like I'd just left reality and escaped into fantasy. I had to ask him, "Is that really your name Officer Buckle?"

"Yes, I know there's a children's book by that title, but it's not named after me. My friends just call me Buck."

"Okay, well I'm Jenna, Mrs. Belmont's only granddaughter. Is there anything we should know before we see her?"

"She's been in and out of consciousness since we found her on the floor in her living room. Her vitals are very weak and she's in shock. But, if she starts talking to you, come out and get me immediately. We have recorders so we can get descriptions of the men who did this to them. Don't worry, Jacob, this is our top priority. Your Grandma and, Jen, your Grandma in there are well respected in these parts. We will find the two hellions who did this. We will bring them to justice."

"Okay thank you officer we'll be out shortly, just guard her door please."

"Granny, it's me under this hospital gown garb, don't be afraid. Can you hear me?"

Granny's eyes were closed, and in her whispery voice she clearly spoke.

"Yes, Jenna, close the door."

I looked at Jacob who is as surprised as I am that she is talking so clearly and calmly. I guess I didn't move quickly enough because my Granny said in a louder whisper.

"Close that damn door now, Jenna!"

I'd never heard my Granny use that kind of language ever before, so I just stood by her bed in shock. Jacob, seeing that my feet weren't moving, quickly moved back over to the door and shut it for me. I didn't tell her Jacob is in the room and he didn't make a sound. I don't know why I didn't say anything about him being with me, it just never occurred to me. I just assumed she'd open her eyes and see us. We had shoe covers over our shoes, so we sort of slid our feet on the floor when walking. That's why Granny probably didn't notice the sound of four feet coming into her room instead of just my two.

"Jenna, move over here by my side quickly and listen closely. I don't have much time to talk to you. I'm only going to say this once, so you need to focus."

I leaned in close, her face so swollen, I hardly recognized her. Jacob is standing directly behind me, keeping his strong arms wrapped around my waist.

"I'm going to tell you exactly what happened. After I do, you get me a lawyer, try to get Sonny Strausz if we can afford him, and tell him everything I'm about to tell you, every word, Jenna. You promise?"

"I promise, Granny. Do you want some pain meds first? Your lip is split open, it looks so painful; and your eye is swollen shut, oh, Granny. If you want to rest until you feel better that's fine, I can wait."

"Jenna, we don't have much time, so for the love of GOD stop talking, listen to me, and do not interrupt me again."

"Okay, Grams, I'm listening."

"That evil woman, she came into my house. No knocking at the door, she just walked in. No, she broke into my home, acting like she owned my place. I told her she needed to leave my house, but she refused. She may own the town and country and everyone in a three-state area, Governors and Senators, but not me, not my land, and not my family, never!"

"I told her to get out of my house again. She had no right to be in my house. She is not invited, and I asked her to leave, but she just sat down and gave me a look, pure evil. She buys and sells people Jenna, has lawyers and politicians in her pockets. She runs this town and every county for three states over, but not me."

I looked back at Jacob knowing he just lost his Grandma, and my Granny is bad mouthing her. Jacob just shook his head like he is telling me no Jenna, just listen to your Grandma.

"Ruth said she came over after all these years, not because she is invited but because she wanted me to know that she and Partner had an affair and that it lasted for over 10 years. That he was the love of her life and that I didn't deserve him. I know it's not true. I have no idea why that woman is so evil; but there she is sitting in my living room, all smug with her attitude, telling me these lies in my own home. I screamed at her, Get Out! Get Out! Get Out!"

Ruth jeered an evil smirk and said, "Your precious Jenna isn't good enough for my favorite and beloved grandson Jacob. Jenna will never have Jacob. I don't share my men anymore, especially with a Belmont. I had to share Partner with you, and there is no way I am going to share Jacob with Jenna.

Jenna and Jacob are going to be history in the near future. I just want you to know who the driving force and power is behind the upcoming break-up. Jenna's a sweet girl, reminds me of her Grandpa, but she will never do for Jacob or any of my kin, she's too common. She's just a teacher, that's what college graduates major in when they can't make it in any other professions to make better money."

"That was it, that's all I could take. I couldn't listen to her lies and controlling lives, not in

my own home, my sanctuary. Something in me just snapped and everything was clearer than it had ever been. I had my fill of her venom for the last time. Years and years of her rubbing me wrong in the same spot and I am raw. Everything moved in slow motion, like I'd planned this for years.

I grabbed my revolver from Partner's end table drawer by my big, overstuffed chair and dropped her right then and there. I couldn't believe I did it. She just lay there, and I panicked. I ran out the front door and kicked the glass out to make it look like intruders. I ran back inside and called 911, told police we had been attacked, and that we needed an ambulance, Ruth had been shot. I wrapped a tea towel around my wrist and hit myself with my left hand, since I'm right-handed. I've watched detective movies on television and remembered that detail. Then I grabbed a baseball bat from behind my front door, hit my ribs several times, and then my head."

"Everything went dark, and I guess I knocked myself out. When I came to, the cops and paramedics were there. I tried to crawl over to Ms. Ruth, to say I was sorry, but nothing would come out. I couldn't speak. The policeman said I was in shock."

"I tried to think of some story I would remember to tell the same way over and over when they started with the questioning. I picked the story of two young men in hoodies that busted in on us. And I grabbed my gun to scare them but the taller one grabbed it from me. Ruth tried to stop them, but he shot her. Then all I remember is seeing Ruth on the floor and they were gone. Did I say black jackets? They were wearing black hooded jackets."

"My God, Granny, you don't know what you are saying." Jacob was squeezing me so tight I could barely breathe. "Granny, open your eyes. Jacob and I are right here and this cannot be true! Say this isn't so!"

Chapter 22

Unbelievable Confession

She opened both eyes immediately, one eye was completely filled with blood and she shut that eye. The other eye was red, swollen and staring directly at Jacob.

Granny growled, "How could you deceive me, Jenna? Why didn't you tell me he was in here with you?"

"I didn't try to deceive you. He flew me out here so I could be with you. He's not the enemy, Granny, he's the man I love. If you want to be mad at someone, how about the woman who just shot and killed his Grandma?"

"Get me my lawyer, Jenna, you promised!" Jacob and I left the room.

"Jacob, wait, before you leave me, let me get my dogs and clothes out of your truck." My heart was beating so hard I thought I was going to have a heart attack. I ran to the elevator to catch up with Jacob. He was tearing off his blue scrubs as he entered the elevator.

Finally catching up with him and pulling off my blue hat and face mask, I half cried, half panted. "I'm so, so sorry, Jacob. I cannot believe this can be true. It's impossible! You know my Granny. This is not her. She must be taking crazy pills. She has been hit in the head, she's not clear, maybe she has a brain tumor. Something is very wrong with her. Partner just died. She has lost her mind Jacob."

"Yeah, Jenna, she just killed my Grandma and admitted it with no regret. I'd say something is very wrong."

I jumped out of the elevator.

"Jenna, stop, just stop. I'm sorry I shouldn't have said that to you. I just need to think. Get back into the elevator. Don't tell another living soul what she just said to you, to us. We have to think. You are staying with me, your dogs are fine. I just need to drive and think. You going with me or staying here with your Granny?"

"Jacob, whatever you want me to do, that's what I'll do. I feel so lost right now."

"Get in my truck and please, Jenna, just don't say a word. I need it quiet so I can think."

I sat in silence, just holding Jacob's hand, my feet up on his dashboard. He didn't even start the truck. We just sat there both staring straight ahead, motionless, wordless, both in shock. What kind of tornado just hit? Finally, after an eternity of silence, my stomach growled loudly. I grabbed my stomach, and Jacob gently put his hand over mine.

"Did you have breakfast or lunch today?"

"Umm no, I didn't have time."

"Jenna, please put on your seatbelt. We'll go get something to eat, and then we can talk this terrible situation out together."

"Jacob, I'm really not hungry and I don't think I could keep anything down anyway."

"You are going to need your strength so you can think clearly and deal with this mess rationally. We need to have clear minds. I'm hungry too, so let's try to eat something and talk through this craziness together."

I felt like I have been beat up and shot, too. My mind is spinning. Did Jacob think I am acting irrational? This cannot be true. My sweet Granny could not be that quick to think of all that stuff, all those details. She is slow and forgetful, how can this have happened? Maybe she is on strong pain killers that are causing her to talk out of her head.

But something about her calm even tone when she was telling me what she did gave me goose bumps on my arms. A sick feeling gnawing in my gut is telling me that she is telling the truth. OMG, she really did kill another human. Oh Ms. Ruth, oh my Jacob. What is he going to do with this information? I should have told Granny he was with me in the hospital room. It all happened so fast. I had no idea she wouldn't open her eyes, or that she would say such shocking, life altering things. I never could have imagined such an awful thing, ever. God, please help Granny, me, and Jacob. I love him, I love my Granny, he loves his Grandma, and he loves me too. How can this be happening? What are we going to do?

Our food came and I didn't have the strength to hold up my spoon for the bowl of soup that Jacob ordered for me. I really think I am in shock. I can't form a clear thought without it evading me like a puff of smoke. What is Jacob thinking, what will he do? What should I do to protect my Granny? She has lost her mind. I should get back to her, but what will I say? What will I do? Jacob and I have to talk but I don't even know where to start? I feel sick all over, maybe there's a bed available next to Granny?

"Jenna?"

Jacob's voice brought my swirling thoughts back to the present.

"Yes?"

"Let's go for a walk."

"You want to go for a walk right now?"

"The fresh air will do us good. I can see you aren't going to make it through your bowl of soup, so we might as well get some fresh air. But you might want to take the crackers, put them in your purse so you can have something to munch on later."

"Okay." How could he be thinking of me and how I'm feeling during a time like this, utter turmoil? It's so refreshing to have a man care about me and show me in ways that are useful and appreciated. I love him.

"Jacob?"

"Yes, Jenna."

"I love you and I'm so sorry about your Grandma and my Granny."

"I love you too. Let me pay the bill and we will walk and talk."

Jacob stood up to pay the bill and I physically couldn't move. I am going to start bawling my eyes out, me who never cries. I summoned all my strength and walked straight for the bathroom. I turned on the water, threw some on my face, and caught a glimpse of my reflection in the mirror. I look pale and like I'd aged ten years since this morning. The tears came rushing down my face, I couldn't stop them. Thank goodness no one is in the bathroom stalls. I heard the bathroom door open. Jacob walked in the women's restroom like he owned the place, took me in his arms, and held me. That made me cry even harder. I couldn't stop crying. I don't want to fall apart, but here I am helpless in Jacob's arms. I feel comforted and loved but lost in what to do. My emotions are trying to catch up with all my confusion, I guess.

I whispered, "Jacob, what are we going to do? I can't even think straight right now. I'm so sorry. I can't believe this. It has to be her meds; she's talking crazy, she's out of her mind. No one in their right mind would take the life of another person. She would never do something like this. She's snapped."

"Creating an insanity plea for her already? No, Jenna, she is telling you the truth, and deep down inside you know it. That's why you and I are in shock right now. I'm here for you, but it is my Grandma she shot and killed. I love my grandma; she was a great woman."

Just then the bathroom door opened, and an older woman looked at us sternly. "So sorry for your loss, Jacob, I heard about Ms. Ruth, and um…kids, I really need to use the restroom. You need to clear out, Jacob."

Jacob took me around my middle and escorted me out of the restroom directly to his truck.

"Jenna, you don't have the energy for a walk, so my truck will have to do for us to process all this out loud. I've been thinking and this is what I've come up with so far.

How about you contact the attorney you promised your Grandma you would, Sonny Strausz. You will need to give him a good-sized retainer fee, because he's the best in the state. You may have to put it on a credit card and let your family work out payments with you down the line. He won't budge on his fees, but he's the best and he knows it. And you'll need his expertise and connections to have a chance to make it through this ordeal."

"I will give you twenty-four hours before I tell my family what I found out from your Granny. Tell your attorney every detail including that I gave you a twenty-four-hour head start into all this before my family with their money and power go for your family's jugular."

"Jenna, they are my family, I feel compelled to tell them what I know. If I didn't, that would always be something that would eat at me until I would resent you. I don't want this to come between us. I hope you understand. I have to tell them the truth. You of all people can respect that right?"

"Jacob, you are amazing! I don't want this to come between us either. I can't even remember my phone number right now, and you have rational thoughts for both of us. Now, can you take me somewhere so I can get a ride?"

"What do you mean? We are in my truck. I can give you a ride wherever you need to go."

"Thank you, but I can't ask you to drive me to the attorney. I don't want to put you in another uncomfortable situation any more than I already have."

"I know attorney Strausz, and if my family hasn't already retained him, you are going to need to do that today. Buckle up Jenna, and I'll take you to his office. If he's not there, I know where he lives."

"I'm so afraid I'll forget something important I'm supposed to tell him. Is there any way you could come inside with me?"

"Jenna! Are you kidding me?"

"I know, I shouldn't ask, but I need you by my side. I'm scared, I don't want to do or say anything or forget anything that will have negative consequences for you and me, our futures, or our families. I need you to just make sure I don't forget some important detail."

Jacob looked deep into my eyes and in a sort of surrender let out his breath like he'd been holding it. "Alright, Jenna, let's go inside."

They approached the receptionist. "Hello, my name is Jenna Lee, and I have an urgent matter to discuss with Attorney Strausz."

"I'm sorry, Ms. Lee, he is just finishing up for the day, I can schedule an appointment for you for…"

"Excuse me, please tell Sonny that Jacob Jamison is here to see him on official business."

"Yes, Mr. Strausz will see you both in the conference room. Care for a drink?"

"Yes, she'll take a Diet Dr. Pepper, and I'll have a Jack and Coke."

"See, Jacob, I told you I needed you."

Mr. Strausz strolled into the large conference room. He

was short, stocky, and balding, but had a welcoming smile. "Jacob, long time no see. And who is this beauty? Is she the fiancée I've heard about? Are you two here for a prenup?"

"No, Sonny. Has my family contacted you to represent them in the death of my Grandma?"

"What? Ms. Ruth is dead? I didn't know. I'm so sorry. She had a brilliant mind for business and money. She will be greatly missed. What can I do for you?"

"Thanks, Sonny. Well, my fiancée Jenna, needs your professional representation for her Grandmother, Mrs. Belmont."

"Sure, I can represent her. Did my secretary discuss my payment rates? Are you able to meet my retainer fees?"

"I will make sure you are paid, sir. Do you need someone to record our conversation or take notes, or should I just tell you the whole truth and nothing but the truth?"

"Jenna, this isn't court, I work for you and anything you tell me is attorney client privilege."

The receptionist returned with their drinks. "Excuse me, here's your Diet Dr. Pepper, and a seasoned Coke for Jacob".

"Thanks, Jackie, I'll let you know if we need anything else. Now Jenna and Jacob, what can I do for you? What's your story?"

"First of all, Mr. Strausz, my Granny is a kind, loving mother of four, and has lots of grandkids, and great grandkids. She's lived in the same house for 50 years, next door to the Jamison family that you are familiar with."

"Anyway, I flew in today to see my Granny. She's in the hospital in ICU and she told me to tell you everything. She requested you by name. She had her eyes closed because her injuries are so severe that it is painful for her to open them. So she didn't know Jacob was in the room with me. She told us everything that happened with the murder of Mrs. Ruth Jamison. And now we are in a terrible mess. It's awful what I'm about to tell you, it is borderline unbelievable.

She said she shot and killed Ms. Ruth. She said Ms. Ruth was controlling and entered her house without permission, so she shot her and then tried to make it look like they had been attacked by intruders. Granny said she beat herself up so bad she passed out. I can't believe it. She may lose her eye and she looks awful."

"But, Mr. Attorney, I mean, Mr. Strausz, when she talked to us, she whispered so the police officer, Mr. Buckle, wouldn't hear her outside her hospital door. She spoke steady and clear like she knew exactly what she was telling me the entire time."

I can't believe this, but Ms. Ruth is dead, and my Granny is in critical condition in the ICU. Jacob has lovingly agreed to give my family twenty-four hours before he tells his family what my Granny told him. Jacob lost his Grandma, and I know he's in a terrible position being here with me, but I trust and love him completely."

"Jacob, I'm going to the hospital to meet Mrs. Belmont. If she isn't going to survive these self-inflicted injuries, then maybe this is a secret we can all take to the grave. Let me assess her condition and ask her some questions. I'll talk to her doctors as well. If she makes improvement, then tell your families. But if she fails, consider this is best, not just for Jenna, but for your family as well, to keep this just between us. I've had experience dealing with these kinds of situations and you are paying me for my professional opinion. I recommend we hold everything in silent mode until we meet back in my office tomorrow."

"No, Mr. Strausz, I'm not asking Jacob to keep the truth from his family, not ever. Don't ask him to do that, it's not fair."

"We are talking about your Grandma's life here, Jenna, not what's fair or even right. And if you want my professional legal advice you sure as hell better take it or there's the door. Do what you want. I play to win, and you need to play by my rules if you want me to work for you."

Jacob spoke up quickly after I unthinkingly squeezed his hand.

"Sonny, you're the professional here, but don't attack the messengers. I'll mull over what you said, but I haven't agreed to anything. I am only here to help Jenna remember everything her Grandma said. And Jenna hasn't told you her Grandma also made up a story she told the police. She told them that two hooded men broke in and she grabbed the gun trying to scare them off. They got her gun from her and shot my Grandma. Mrs. Belmont ran to the front door and busted out the glass, then beat herself unconscious."

"I realize this puts you in a terrible position, Jacob. I will do my best to represent your fiancée's Grandma, but you are on the opposing side if your family files a suit against Mrs. Belmont. And knowing your family, like I do know your family, you better prepare yourselves for an all-out war. If the truth of this gets out, both of you better get ready for world war three."

"I need to call my wife and tell her I won't be home for dinner. Then I'm headed to the hospital. Ms. Jenna you can no longer discuss this case with your fiancé. You will only make things worse for him and for your Grandmother if you don't do what I tell you to do. That's why you are paying me. I do this every day and I work to win all my cases. I am the best and I take my winning record very seriously. So, don't 'F' with me. Just do what I tell you to do and I will take care of this for you and your family."

"I don't appreciate the unprofessional language, Mr. Strausz. I'm paying you to represent my Grandmother, not to disrespect me. You drop that 'F' bomb on me again, Mr. Attorney, you will see an explosion you don't want to mess with. Do I make myself perfectly clear? I may be upset and frazzled right now, but I am a professional and educated woman. You will talk to me with respect."

"You're clear. I'm sorry I misspoke. Anything else?"

"Yes, here's my cell number if you need to contact me. Should Jacob and I go back to the hospital too?"

"Jacob, I'll take Jenna. You should stay away."

"Thank you for representing Jenna and her family, Sonny. I have her clothes and her dogs. Mrs. Belmont's house is roped off as a crime scene, so Jenna is staying with me."

"Oh no, she's not doing that. That is not an option. You two are not to be together until this is over. That is my strong professional recommendation. I'm just trying to make this easier for both of you. I'm sorry you both got thrown in the middle of this, but here you are and apart you will stay until this matter is settled"

"Unless…. You know there's another option. If you and Jenna are married, a wife can't testify against her husband, and the husband can't testify against his wife. Just something to think on if you two can't stay away from each other."

"Now, I need to go see my new client. I'll give you two a minute while I make a few phone calls, then Jenna you can ride with me back to the hospital. You two can talk in here. I'll have Jackie call the room, when I'm ready to leave and we can meet at the front door."

Jenna shook his hand. "Thank you, Mr. Strausz."

"Just call me Sonny."

"Okay, thank you, Sonny."

Chapter 23

Learning the Truth

"Jacob, I'm so sorry for putting you in the middle of all of this. I should have never asked you to go with me to see my Granny. I was way out of line to ask you to come in here with me this afternoon, and yet I needed your wisdom and strength. I am better with you. You continue to put my needs above your own, and I'll never forget how you showed me how much you loved me by doing this today. I know this isn't easy for you. Please don't worry about me. I am okay now. I am stronger than I look and I will get through this. I think I sort of temporarily lost it because I feel so safe with you."

"I think I knew I could fall apart because I had someone I trusted by my side to be strong when I was weak. Thank you for letting me be imperfect through this living nightmare. But most of all thank you for loving me. I love you so much."

"I love you too. You need to listen and do exactly what

Sonny advises. He's right. We need to keep a low profile until the heat of this blows over. You have no idea what this will be like when my family finds out your Granny killed my Grandma. Your mom and her siblings will be here soon. They can help you and you can help them. Ask Sonny if you should tell them what you know. You can trust Sonny he's the best money can buy."

"I'm not telling anyone anything. The attorney knows, and he is responsible to protect my Granny. I was responsible to get Granny her attorney. My job is done."

"She killed your Grandma. I loved your Grandma too. I want to be there for you, like you've been here for me. I'm not on trial here, and neither are you. We have done nothing wrong, unless you count the video footage from the hospital parking lot. If we want to be together, we can be together. I can't imagine being this close to you and not holding you in my arms. I love you. You've been here for me, what can I do for you?"

"How about oral sex?"

"What?"

"I was just trying to lighten the mood, but the look on your face is so worth it. Babe, we need to stay clear of each other like Sonny said. We can hook up at night, somehow, someway, we will be together. If we promise each other we won't talk about our Grandmas, we could be together. I will take your dogs out to my place and they will be safe inside my house. When you are ready to go back to Missouri, I will bring your dogs, and drive you to the airport myself."

"Jenna, another thought, don't text me anything you don't want read in an open courtroom setting. E-mail is a public domain and emails between us cannot talk about either of our Grandmas. I'm sorry to lay down all the restrictions, but I'm thinking of you. I'm trying to protect you and us from future potential problems if this goes to court.

I know my family and what they are capable of doing

and your family will need to follow the good advice of your attorney at every single turn, or my family will eat your family alive."

"That's my Jacob, always thinking. Thank you for being you. That sounds so Hallmark cards, but I really appreciate your mind as well as your body. Please tell me your body will be next to mine tonight?"

The office phone rang and Jacob answered. "That is Jackie, she said the attorney is ready to leave for the hospital."

"It's okay. We will be together soon. I will text you when I'm free to talk tonight, but it might be late. And when you are alone and can talk, text me back that you love me. Then I'll know I can call you and we can talk freely from there. I love you, Jenna. No matter how this all turns out, always know I love you now and forever."

There was a knock at the door. "Ms. Jenna, I'm on the clock and you're paying. I'm ready when you are."

"Alright then let's go."

Jacob opened the door and walked with me out to the attorney's passenger side door. "Buckle up and drive safe you two. You're caring for my future wife, Sonny."

"Love you. Love on my dogs for me, they need half a cup of dog food in the morning and in the evening same amounts. Oh, and they fight, so they need to be spaced apart when you feed and water them. Thanks, and good-bye for now, my Jacob."

"I'll take good care of the Belmont family. You lay low Jacob, and remember twenty-four hours or more depending on Mrs. Belmont's recovery rate. Just think about what I said and take care."

I didn't have a ride to a hotel until two hours later. Mom and Thomas were spending the night at the hospital with Granny. Dwayne was driving me and Elaine to the hotel. Elaine and I are sharing one room with double beds, and Dwayne has another double bedroom that Thomas and he will share while taking shifts sleeping and being at the hospital with Granny. Dwayne dropped me off at the hotel, but Elaine and Dwayne wanted to drive out and see Granny's house before they can go to sleep. They wanted to make sure it was safe and secure.

I got a text from Jacob. "I miss you." When I reached my room, I texted Jacob, "I love you with my whole heart!" My phone rang seconds later.

"Hi, babe, how you holding up?"

"Okay, Jacob, and you?"

"I must have fallen asleep. Where are you?"

"I'm at the hotel down the block from the hospital. Elaine will be back in the room in about an hour or so. The girls are all staying in one room and the boys in the next room. Mom and Thomas are staying at the hospital with Granny. How about you and your family?"

"Grandma has a will and all her wishes are being carried out to the letter. She wouldn't have had it any other way. Everyone is on edge and at each other's throats wondering who gets what in the almighty will. Nice family you are marrying into, huh?"

"I'm so sorry that you have to go through any of this at all. You sound so tired. Baby, get some sleep, I'm tired too. We can communicate same way tomorrow."

"Jenna, we are going to see each other tomorrow, even if I have to marry you to do it."

"I know Sonny mentioned that option but I don't want to marry you to get out of something. I only want to marry you to get into your heart, life, your bed, and your future. Wait a minute someone's at my door, just a minute."

"What do you mean someone is at your hotel door? At this time of night? No one should be knocking at your door, look through the peep hole, don't open the door. Do you know who it is?"

"Jacob," I whispered. "It's your brother Andrew. What should I do?"

"Do not open your door, Jenna! What the hell is he doing at your hotel room at this time of the night? How does he know where you are? Do not let him in. He should know it's late and you are sleeping."

Knock... knock... knock... a little louder this time. "Jenna, it's me, Andrew. Let me in!"

"Jacob, he wants me to let him inside".

"Do not let him in your room, I'm hanging up the phone so I can call him. I'll talk to you tomorrow."

I heard Andrew's phone ring on the other side of my hotel door, "Jacob, I know but I wanted to talk to her without you being all watch dog over her. No, I can talk to whomever I choose and right now I'm going to make a ruckus unless Jenna lets me in her room." He began yelling. "Jenna, let me in. I'm not quieting down until you let me inside. JENNA!"

I don't know what he wanted but it was late, I am exhausted, and Elaine will have a literal fit if some hot guy is in my hotel room when she gets here, so there is no way I am letting him in. Besides Jacob said not to let him in.

I got on my hotel phone and called down to the front desk. "There is a drunk in the hallway outside my room yelling. Please come get him before he wakes the entire floor." Moments later I heard low voices and Andrew left yelling at the top of his lungs "Jenna. You and me later, Jenna."

What in the world could be so important that he needs to talk to me at this time of night? I called Jacob back on my cell, he sounded madder than I've ever heard him.

"I'm almost at your hotel, where's Andrew?"

"I'm not exactly sure. The hotel security came to take him away from my door. He was yelling disturbing the guests. I had to call the front desk before the whole floor was awake."

"That is good thinking on your part. Andrew never has been able to handle his liquor. He's taking Grandma's death really hard. I'll drive him home. Jen, you okay?"

Jacob has never called me Jen before. I've never liked my name shortened, but when Jacob called me Jen, I loved it. For the first time ever. "I must be really tired, babe. I've lost all track of time and space. That happens a lot to me when I'm around you. Are you buckled up and driving safe?"

"I'm buckled up but driving as fast as I can to get to my brother. What time are you getting up?"

"I'm not sure, I think my family will eat breakfast together at the hotel, and then switch with Mom and Thomas, so they can sleep, eat, take showers, etc. Now that they are all here, I want to let them take the lead and I plan to slip into the background on this huge mess."

"Well, if you're eating in the morning with your family, I'll try to meet you for lunch. We can eat at the hospital lunchroom or I'll take you somewhere that sounds better. When you get hungry, text me and I'll come get you. I'm here at the hotel now. Good Lord, you should see the way Andrew parked his truck. Clearly, he's been drinking. I'll talk to you tomorrow, Jenna. Love you."

I would have said love you too, but he'd already hung up his phone. He's tired, I'm exhausted, and it's only 10:57. It feels like midnight or later. I don't know when Elaine got in, but I didn't hear a thing.

I didn't hear her when she got up the next morning, took a shower, and went downstairs with Dwayne for breakfast. I woke when my hotel room door opened and it was Mom. She is coming to sleep for a few hours. Her back is killing her from sitting in the hospital chair all night. She wanted to shower and rest then we are all going to eat dinner together tonight.

"What time is it mom?"

"It's 11:00."

"Why didn't someone wake me up? You use the restroom if you need it mom, but I'm jumping in the shower. I'll be grabbing a bite with Jacob, then I'll meet you at the hospital later. How's Granny?"

"Honey, she's an eighty-six year old woman and was beaten by two young thugs. She hasn't improved, but she's not worse either. We take what we can get. With dad just passing away, I hope mom has the strength to fight to get better. She's emotionally fragile right now."

"Well, that's sort of good news that she's not worse." I felt so much better after a hot shower and clean clothes. I texted Jacob. *I am starving!*

He won't have to ask me to eat today because I'm all about the food. I used to be fat. After I got married, I was pretty much rejected by the man who was supposed to want me, so food became my non-judgmental friend and companion. Only after my divorce did I slowly begin to believe I was worth the effort to be fit and healthy again.

I'm no skinny Minnie and never will be. I have my curves and I'm proud of them, that's how I roll... ha ha. Self-image humor, fat and on a roll. Too bad no one else knows how funny I am. Or maybe it's just I'm the only one who thinks I'm funny. Oh well, I'm happy with who I am and how I look now. That's been a lifetime coming, but Jacob has seen me naked and still wants me, so how could I not feel good about myself after that? I'm just so focused on him that I don't think about me and all my physical flaws, it's a good feeling to be blinded by love. I do love that man. He's been nothing but wonderful through this whole mess!

"Babe, I'm at the front door, should I come up to the room?"

"No, mom's here, and I don't trust us in a hotel room together."

"Good point. Meet me in the lobby."

One step off of the elevator and I was in his arms. My legs wrapped around his waist. My hands grabbing handfuls of his hair, our lips pulsating with passion. Oh, my

Jacob, I missed the taste of him, the strength of him next to me. God did a perfect job with him. He is so handsome, he melts me at a glance of him. He smelled so good, it is all I could do to not rip his clothes off right then and there. Jacob probably would have been fine with that, but if I'm moving to this area, I have to think of our future in this community. I need to act respectable.

"Jacob, stop, we need to go eat. Have you eaten today?"

He looked at me weird. "Yes, I had breakfast. And you?"

Darn that conversation didn't go where I wanted it to. "No, so let's go someplace close because seriously I'm very hungry."

"You have crackers in your purse from yesterday, remember?"

"Oh yeah, thanks for reminding me, you want one?"

"No thanks. Any lunch requests?"

"Nope, just something close, I don't care."

"Okay then how about we go to an Italian restaurant. Does that sound good to you?"

"Sure. Baby, when you are hungry anything sounds good. Can we get a dark corner booth somewhere and make out while we wait for our food?"

"No, folks know me around here and that's not behavior they are used to seeing. And under the current circumstances we don't want the rumor mill to add to the fire that will be spreading when the word gets out about our Grandmas."

"You're right. I know, I am being selfish. I just want you all the time. It's totally inescapable; you are the love of my life. You are a dream I never would have dreamed for myself because I never believed I deserved anyone as wonderful as you. I am in constant shock that you could be in love with me, Jacob, because I love you so desperately. I'm afraid I'm going to wake up and you will be gone, and all I'll have is the memory of my dream. You make me so happy."

"You make it very difficult for me to keep my distance from you when you pour out your heart in this loving vulnerable way you have about you. I love you and we have to change the subject, or this town will be talking about this day and our time together in this very booth for a very long time."

"Baby, I feel your pain, so consider the subject changed."

"Speaking of baby, how's your car?"

"Our car is fine. Way to change the subject, you are so smooth. Hey how's your brother today? And what in the world did he want to talk to me about so urgently last night?"

Before he could answer the waitress came over. "Your order?"

"Yes, we will have two orders of lasagna, side salad, one with blue cheese the other Italian dressing and a large Diet Dr. Pepper and a large Coke, and two waters. Anything I missed babe?"

"Nothing except I would appreciate it if we could have our salads early. That would be fabulous. Thanks."

"Yum, homemade bread with oil and spices, please stop me if I'm making a pig of myself. I don't want to embarrass myself or you, but those crackers didn't do a thing for me. After the delicious meal, I sat back in my chair to breathe, and the look on Jacob's face is priceless. He looked like he is ready to crack up.

"Honey, you should eat every meal, so you aren't so starved. Seriously, if you eat that fast you will die. You ate your food in like world record time." I looked at his plate. He still had more than half his food and I'd eaten almost the whole loaf of bread, a salad, and my main course. Oink, oink, once again he sees me at my worst. Way to go, Jenna.

"Sorry, but in my defense I'm an elementary teacher and I have thirty minutes for lunch. In that time I have to walk my kids all the way to their lunch room, then use the restroom, stand in line to cook my lunch in one of the two microwaves in the teachers' lounge, and then in the few minutes remaining, I get to eat my lunch and walk back down to get my kids. It's a terrible way to eat, but if I didn't eat fast, I wouldn't get lunch at school every day. Sorry if I embarrassed you, I'm not thinking. However, I'll work on slowing down my inhaling food in public."

"You take your time and enjoy your food, don't feel like you need to eat quickly. I'll sit here and try to regain my composure and enjoy my view of handsome you. And just so you know, I noticed that you haven't answered my question about Andrew and his urgency to talk to me last night."

"I don't understand the look you're giving me. If this is family stuff and I am prying, don't tell me. But he did come to me, and if we hadn't been on the phone at the time, I would have let him in my room. But only because he's your brother and he sounded like he was desperate."

Jacob put down his fork and looked even more furious with me. Then he spoke in a low, even tone. "Jenna, if you ever are stupid enough to open your door to a drunken man at that time of night, I'll, I'll…"

Defensively I asked, "You'll do what, Jacob?"

"I'll be by your side, so I guess I'll be kicking some ass in the middle of the night. You have better sense than to open your hotel room to a drunken man. Don't ever do that, ever!"

"Wait a minute, are you telling me by not telling me, that your brother wanted a booty call from me? Last night? Are you kidding me? He knows you and I are together."

"He had a rough day, you are hot, he was drunk and upset. He knew you were in town when he heard your dogs barking at my house. But he's okay today, except for that massive headache he's nursing."

My phone rang. "It's a text from Dwayne. Granny is

asking to see you and me together as soon as possible. What should we do?"

"Get the check and go see your Granny."

"But the attorney, Jacob... if you are okay with doing this, then I am too, let's go."

Chapter 24

Final Remarks

"Granny we are here, Jacob and I are here like you requested."

I am not taking any chances that she isn't aware that Jacob is with me this time. Even though she's the one who requested we both come to see her, I didn't want to make the same mistake twice.

"Would the rest of you please leave the room, I need to speak to these two love birds privately."

"You sure, Mom? Is everything okay?"

"Yes, my precious, Thomas. You kids go down to the cafeteria and get some nourishment. I want to talk to my only granddaughter and her fiancé."

"Okay, Granny, they're all gone now. What is it you'd like to say to us?"

"Please shut the door so we can have some privacy."

Oh great, here it comes. Granny can't write a letter so she's going to give it to me face to face. She knows I won't say anything back. Jacob took my hand and we walked closer to her bed side. I thought she would look better today, but she looked more swollen, yet smaller and frailer than I'd ever seen her. I was so busy being mad at her for losing her mind and for killing Ms. Ruth that I didn't stop to think I could lose her for good from all of this. She is eighty-six years old and just lost her lifelong mate just weeks earlier.

"Granny, what is it you want to tell us?"

"I need to say some things to you two and I want you to be quiet and listen. Don't interrupt, Jenna."

Like anyone could ever get a word in edgewise with Granny. Granny always did like things done her way, so why should now be any different?

"Okay, shoot. No wait, you already did that."

"I deserved that comment, Jacob. I just want you both to know that I am eternally sorry for what I did. I cannot believe I did such an unforgivable thing. I've told my attorney to plead guilty to first degree murder. I had no right to take the life of anyone, no matter how long she was a thorn in my flesh. I don't want my actions in any way to stand between the two of you and your happiness. I have tried to figure out what made me do it, and I honestly believe I temporarily lost my mind, if that is even possible. I would never hurt anyone on purpose, and I'm really shocked and feel like someone else did this horrible thing. I'm so sorry, Jacob, for the loss of your Grandma. I've never even killed an animal before, I hate guns. I don't know why I did it. It was like I was watching someone else do it. But it was me, all me. I can't change it, but every fiber of me is sorry."

"Now, Jenna, I've talked to you on the phone over the last month and you've come alive since you've been with Jacob. Tom nearly killed you. He literally sucked the life out of you, and I wondered if you'd ever come back to be the woman we all knew and loved.

But with Jacob, I see a joy in your demeanor, a twinkle in your eyes that quite honestly, I've never seen before. Life is too short you two, so don't look for an excuse to give up on love. You are a Belmont, Jenna, fight for what you want!

Love is worth fighting for; wars have been fought, won and lost for much less. Fight for your right to be happy together. Always respect one another and listen to not just the words, but the heart behind the words. You two can have happily ever after, I just know it. Don't let my temporary insane moment take away your future for happiness. I love you both. I'm so sorry."

"My future will include recovery, then directly to prison. I didn't need my big house anymore anyway, too much to keep clean. Three meals a day delivered to my private room, prisons have room service and free dental and medical. I will be fine. There isn't anything that could happen to me there that I haven't already done to myself. I don't understand why I did what I did. I keep asking myself over and over and nothing, just an empty blackness. And I'm ready to take full responsibility for my actions."

"Jacob, again I have no words except I'm so sorry, but don't hold this against Jenna, she loves you. I've loved you too, like extended family. You are the best thing that ever came from Ms. Ruth. I am so sorry for my actions and the pain it must be causing your family."

"My attorney will meet with my kids at 4:00 today and tell them what happened, and my decision on how to proceed with legal actions. I don't know for sure, but I'm thinking my kids will try to have me declared mentally incompetent, and then I'll be sent off to a loony bin. Before all of the consequences come crashing down on me and my family, I just wanted to have one last moment with the two of you to say again how very sorry I am. If I could take it back I would. I wish it would have been me and not your Grandma that died that day. I know my words are so small, but I mean them from a lifetime of good followed behind one split second act of losing it."

"Granny, I love you, always have, always will. Love is unconditional. Good or bad, stupid or crazy. We are family and I'm here for you, whatever you need."

"The truth, embrace the truth, always. No matter how much it hurts at first, it will always give you a solid foundation to stand on. It's secure, it will sustain you through life's storms. Don't sidestep the truth to try to protect me, or anyone. I will be fine whatever my fate may be. Now kids, I need to rest, I'm not feeling well."

"Alright we'll let you rest. Love you, Granny."

"Love you too, Jenna, and, Jacob."

"Thanks for your apology, Mrs. Belmont. I will forgive you in time, but right now, all I can see is a beat-up old woman, a woman I thought I knew. A woman who stole my flesh and blood, injuring me with hollowness inside what used to be filled with my Grandma.

As controlling as she could be, she didn't deserve an ending like that, you shot her and left her to bleed to death. I need to know, did she die immediately or lay there and struggle for each and every breath?"

"No, no, Jacob, it wasn't like that. She was gone almost immediately. No anguish or suffering. She had a quick ending. When I came to my senses, I tried to get to her, to stop the bleeding, but I was too late."

"I'm not going to say those three words you want me to say so you can rest easier at night. You want honest, there it is. I love your granddaughter, and I will take good care of her. So, if that gives you comfort, that's all I'm capable of doing for you at this point."

"Jacob, my dear boy, that's all I would ever want for my kids to be healthy and happy. I love you both very much and will always have a special place in my heart for both of you. Now go, I really need rest. I'm not feeling well."

We stepped away from the bed and walked over to open

the door. I was holding Jacob's hand and my heart was breaking for both of them. My mom and aunt and uncles walked in the room and we were about to leave, but then it happened.

Granny's machines started going off with loud alarms. It was familiar sounds I'd heard not too long ago, with all the bells and whistles as I watched my dad take his last breath from the theft of cancer. I heard "code blue" over the intercom and Granny's ICU room number. Then nurses ran in, my mom, her sister and brothers scooted away from Granny's bedside so the nurses could meet her needs. I remember just stepping back too so they could get to her.

No way could she be leaving us. She's the one that beat herself up. How is it possible that she killed herself? This nightmare just won't end. Why aren't they pounding on her chest? I'm waiting for them to do their job but nothing, I couldn't take it anymore. I blurted out with surprising volume, "Why aren't you pounding her chest?"

"I'm sorry, ma'am, she has a do not resuscitate order on her chart. We are not allowed to bring her back."

"Well then get out of my way, because I'm going to pound the life back into her." Just then I saw the looks of shock and disbelief on my mom and her sibling's faces. Oh, dear God! They have no idea what has really happened. They just lost their dad, now their mom. Jacob put his arm around my waist and guided me out of the room.

"Jenna, your family needs to say goodbye to their mom in peace. Not with you on top beating the hell out of her. I appreciate your fight baby, but you know this is her best way out, and she knew it too. Let her go in peace. She's asked forgiveness and made things right with her maker, let her go."

"Oh, Jacob..." I just turned and held my face into his chest. Thank you for being my voice of reason throughout this heart wrenching nightmare. I couldn't survive this without you. Seriously, I don't know why you would want to stay with me after all you've been privy to. I have not been the strong independent woman I pride myself on being, I don't know... I just don't know... No, I do know, I love you Jacob, forever. And I can promise you this, if that was you on that bed, I would have been on top of you pounding your chest until I couldn't pound anymore or until you were breathing on your own. I would never give you up."

"I believe you. I'm sure in time we will see this with perspective, and we'll be able to move past all this. But in the meantime, if you're able, you need to call Sonny, tell him what's happened so he doesn't tell your family. They will never need to know the truth."

My uncle Dwayne walked up to us at that moment, "Know what? What did mom say to you two with her dying breath?"

I was shocked that he would ask us that. It's a natural question but he's not the prying type, so it really caught me off guard. I just stood there unable to speak. So once again it was Jacob to the rescue.

"Oh, she told us life is short, and that we should love one another. It took her a while to get all those words out. Now seeing they were her last words, it's understandable that she didn't say a lot to us. I know she loved you all very much and I'm so sorry for your loss."

"Jacob, we are so sorry for the loss of your Grandma too. We will do everything in our power to find the two men who did this to our families. No elderly couple is sleeping sound anymore since they've heard of the break in and murders of our loved ones. They will be caught. Someone will pay for taking the lives of our family members. People are actually locking their doors now. Can you believe it?"

"Oh my gosh, I can't do this. I'm sorry all. I know you just buried your dad, and now here's your mom, my granny. It's been two years since my dad died, and I still can't handle the hospital and death scene. I love you all, but I've got to get out of here, I need some fresh air." Dwayne patted Jacob on the shoulder and said "I'll take care of Jenna's mom. You take care of you and Jenna."

I was already to the elevator and had my cell phone out, "Sonny, we need to talk immediately. Granny just died. I thought the family could rest easy not knowing the truth, but I can't live with that lie. They have to have full disclosure, the truth, the whole truth, and nothing but the truth. They don't need to spend their time and money looking for two men in hoodies who don't even exist. That is just wrong. You have to tell them everything, today. Give them a couple of hours or so to pull themselves together, but you have to tell them so they can make informed decisions about their futures."

I received a text back from Sonny. "Ms. Jenna, as per your Grandmother's instruction, that is exactly what I will do at 4:00 p.m. today. You can be there when this conversation occurs or not, it's up to you. Oh, and Mrs. Belmont said she is paying my bill and to tell you not to charge things on such a high interest thing as a credit card. For an eighty-six-year-old woman, who was beaten so badly, she had spunk. I've got to go, see you or not at 4:00."

"Yeah, that sounds like Granny. She asks you to do something, and then tells you that you didn't do it the way she would have done it. That's Granny to the very end."

"Jacob, can we go to your place or do you need to be somewhere with your family?"

"We can go to my place and rest for a while then I'll take you back to the hotel for the meeting if you want to be there for that discussion."

"Home sweet home, where's my Molly and Moose? Molly, Moose? Jacob, where are my puppies?"

"Damn it, Andrew must have let them out and forgot to let them back inside. We'll find them, don't worry, babe."

I flew out of Jacob's front door yelling for my Molly and Moose. I walked on every side of the four-sided deck and hollered with my outside recess voice for my playful puppies. No barking sounds, no floppy ears running toward me, nothing. I just stared at Jacob I couldn't take any more loss. I couldn't even shed a tear. I just stared at him. My Dad, my Partner, my Granny, my dogs, people and pets, those I love die... I'm alone. My legs just folded up underneath me and I dropped to the ground.

"Jenna, honey I'll find your dogs. This is a farm with lots of new smells for them. They are together and having a blast somewhere close. I'm sure they are fine. I will find them. Don't worry, babe, it's going to be okay. Let me get a hold of Andrew on the phone. Let me help you in the house so you can get something to eat or drink. Here sit in this chair."

"Andrew, I'm at the house with Jenna. Where are her dogs? Jenna's granny just died and she comes here for her dogs and they're gone too. What? Chick magnets? Get your ass and those dogs back to this house now! What is wrong with you lately Andrew? Pull your head out and get Jenna's dogs back to my place."

"Jenna, sweetheart, Molly and Moose are alive and well. They are in Andrew's truck with him. He thinks they're cute, so he got the wild idea that they would help him attract women. He thinks they are chick magnets. He said they are doing a great job for him and he might have to get one for himself. I'm not kidding. I couldn't make this up if I tried. It's never boring with you Jenna, never. But he's bringing your dog's back to the house now. It's going to be okay, they are both fine."

"Oh, thank God, Jacob, thank God. I couldn't lose one

more thing, not today. Andrew may be in danger of his life when I get a hold of him, but hopefully he's far enough away that I'll cool down before I see him."

"Now are we okay? If after all this, after all that's happened, if you need to cut your losses, and let me go, now's the time to do it. I'll do all my grieving and depression at once. Remember, honesty. Just rip the Band-Aid off quickly. Don't make this a long, drawn out, painful goodbye."

"Seriously, why are you scrunching your shoulders and squeezing your eyes shut? I love you. And honestly the more I think about you wanting to climb up on your Granny and pound the life back into her, it makes me love you that much more. I want you fighting in my corner, for me and for us forever. You are not a loss. You are a treasure. I've never been happier than since I've been with you. I could have done without your Granny killing my Grandma, but as far as you and I are concerned, my feelings haven't changed. I love you."

"How much time do we have before Andrew is here?"

"Don't tempt me."

"Tempt, you have no idea, I haven't begun to tempt you."

"We've got twenty minutes tops."

"Okay then."

I raced up the stairs to beat Jacob to his bedroom. But he was skipping two stairs at a time. This stupid cast is a handicap. That's when Jacob scooped me into his arms and carried me to the bedroom, our sanctuary from the crazy world around us.

No matter what happened out there, we had us. All this crazy and we are still together, a team. This is the way I always dreamed it could be. I can't believe how much I need him, how much I crave him. I can't believe that he loves me. I have my Jacob and he definitely has me, all of me. Love never meant so much to me as it does now. Jacob has thrown me into a category of love I've never know before. And I'm staying with him.

Chapter 25

The Departure

Even before their bodies were laid to rest, the attorneys were scheduling meetings with the loved ones to read the last will and testaments of our dearly departed Grandmas.

By now both families had talked to their respected attorneys and all knew the truth, the whole truth about what happened between our Grandmothers. My family was being sued by Jacob's family and it is going to be a long, expensive nightmare to say the least.

Since I'm a grandchild, I am out of the immediate daily drain and drama of this ordeal. My mom and her siblings will manage all the attorney meetings, court dates, newspaper articles, and find the money to keep Granny's expensive attorney paid.

Jacob's dad is the primary executor on his mother's estate. He is also the one not speaking to me or my family and telling us his lawyers will be in touch. But in a small town the news spreads fast and the rumor mill is in full rotation.

Jacob is taking a lot of pressure from his family and friends for being in a relationship with me, the murderous enemy. Even to the point that one of the enlightened few said if it wasn't for me and Jacob, this would have never happened between our Grandmas.

Really, this is all our fault? It's easy to blame others when you're upset and hurting. You have no idea how hard it is for me to keep my mouth shut and not defend Jacob twenty-four seven, but Jacob said he knows his family and my words will just fuel the fire. I just needed to be still and let things work out in time. Did the Hatfield's and McCoy's live in Kentucky, just wondering?

I offered and wanted to go with Jacob to his Grandma's funeral, but he said it would be worse for him if I was there, so I should stay away. I didn't ask him to go to my Granny's funeral. My family is raw with emotion and the Jamison's are taking advantage of this murder to get public sympathy so that they can ultimately get the land and house my Grandparents homesteaded half a century ago. My Granny and Partner worked hard all their lives to leave the land and savings to their kids. Now, they are gone and so will be all that they ever had. It's so tragic! My heart breaks.

After the funerals, Granny's estate was frozen due to the legal litigation against her from the Jamison family. I suggested that we just take the pictures from the house and any keepsakes then give all the land, house, buildings, livestock to the Jamison's and say it's over. I got glairing eyes my way. Guess I need to be silent with my family too. They do know how difficult that task is for me, nearly impossible, but I had to just shut up and let them deal with the legal details.

Jacob called and wanted me to come over to his place. I

told him I'd be free in an hour or so. His voice sounded strained and I asked him if he is alright. He said he's fine and he'd see me soon. When I got to Jacobs house, he seemed cold and distant toward me. Even the tone of his voice sounded different, almost business like, not full of love and strength like I'm used to hearing from him.

"When are you going back home? Now that the funeral is over, I thought you could go back home, get back to your normal routine, and let things cool off around here. I am torn wanting to be with you, but my family is shocked and hurting and you can't be around right now without adding to their pain. We need to be apart for a while. My feelings haven't changed for you, I love you, but I think this will be best for both of us."

"I understand."

"Wow, a two-word response from Jenna, that can't be good, not from you."

"Yep."

"Down to one word. You're not going to shoot me now are you, Jenna?"

"Wow that's a low blow. You want words, oh I'll give you words Jacob Jamison! I can't believe you just said that I might shoot you. Are you kidding me? After what we've just been through… your Grandma said she would separate us, and you are going to let her do that from beyond the grave.

Are you always going to think that since my Granny killed your Grandma, that I could be capable of doing something that terrible too? You are going to believe that my family owes your family. That debt can never be repaid, we can't bring the dead back to life. If I had the power to do it, I'd bring back Ms. Ruth, but it's not possible.

Jacob we can't make "sorry" cover the taking of a life. I don't know how to make this better. It comes down to trust and by the choice of your words, I don't think you trust me anymore, and that sweetheart, is breaking my heart. You don't need to worry about me adding stress to you or your family. You've never been cruel to me before now, but when you do hit, it's below the belt."

"I'm not your verbal punching bag. You can't use your words as a tool to hurt me. I love you and your words mean more to me than anyone else's. Emotional swings can hurt more than physical hits. You want to hit me? Bring it on, hit me! You want me gone, I'm out of here. I won't allow myself to be anyone's pain dispenser. I love you and I don't want to fight with you. But you were unkind with your words. Do you have anything you want to say to fix this? Now's the time; you wanted words; I gave them to you, honest communication. So, what do you have to say to me now?"

"Jenna, you should go."

"That's it, that's all you have to say to me? How about telling me 'No, I'm sorry, Jenna, I know you and I love you and I didn't mean those mean words'. I'd love to hear that from you. Hello…Anything?"

"Like I said, Jenna, you need to go back home."

"You don't love me anymore? Jacob? Okay have it your way." *My heart is racing and I can't think straight. What just happened? He said one unkind thing and I just blew it out of proportion and now he's asked me to leave. Molly, Moose, suitcase in hand, making several trips down his stairs, unassisted by Jacob. And him, not a word, not I'm sorry Jenna, I didn't mean it, I love you too, don't go. Just silence. The quiet was deafening.*

I called Jeff. He is here for the funeral too, and I told him he had to pick me up as soon as he could possibly get to Jacobs because I just got dumped and I don't want to fall apart in front of him.

"Jenna, are you alright?"

"No absolutely in no way am I alright! Jeff, please just get here before he sees that he's destroyed me to my core. I can't cry in front of him, Jeff, I can't. You've got to come get me now. I've got my suitcase and my dogs. Help me, Jeff, please come quickly. I can't talk anymore, I'll lose it."

I was sitting out on the front steps of his deck and Jacob was standing behind me. I could feel his eyes burning holes in the back of my head, but I refused to look at him, refused to say a word. I have to maintain no eye contact, no verbal, or I'll ball like a baby.

I have to leave the man I love. The man I thought loved me as much as I love him. But when things got tough, he took his family's side over the truth of me, of us. I'm trying to think and pray that God will help me, so I don't get sick right here and now.

I don't know where Jeff was at the time of my call, but he must have broken speed barriers, because fifteen minutes later he is jumping out of his rental and running to the porch. I had both my pet carriers, suitcase, and as long as I didn't have to speak, I could hold back the tears. I saw Thomas and Dwayne in the back seat of the car, looking ready at the first sign to jump out and punch Jacob.

I had to keep myself together for a peaceful ending. I didn't want my family in any more legal trouble with Jacob's family and definitely not on my account. In order to survive, I knew I just needed to get out of his presence as quickly as possible. Jeff grabbed my suitcase and told me to get in the car, and he'd get the dogs. I am afraid he'd say something to Jacob, but I had to get to the car before I fell apart.

Jeff grabbed my dogs and loaded them in the trunk. I didn't want them in there, but it is a short drive and I had to pick my battles at that moment. My dogs will be fine there for a short drive. Then here comes Jacob, standing, no he was leaning against the post on his deck. He is acting like he's out enjoying the beautiful weather, not like he has just kicked me out of his life without remorse. I am seeing a man I didn't even know. How could he act this way toward me after all we have shared? What have I done to deserve this treatment? How can this be happening now?

"I see Jenna's rescue squad made it here in record time, what a shocker. Good luck with this little lady, she's a handful. It takes an entire extended family to keep her in line. Do you guys get paid for your positions, or is it on a volunteer basis?"

"Jacob, we are leaving we don't want any trouble."

Thomas and Dwayne opened their back doors of the car and stood up. I thought I was going to faint. Please God just keep the tempers down so we can leave without verbal or physical violence. We've seen enough of that with our Grandmother's!

I could tell Jeff determined things were escalating quickly, so he spoke again in a calm tone.

"I warned her that she was making a big mistake with you, and I guess I should thank you for proving me right, before you got a ring on her finger. Thank you for showing your true colors."

Then Jeff and the boys got back into the car and drove me away, away from my Jacob. My whole body started shaking uncontrollably. I thought I was having some kind of seizure or fit or something. I was freezing, and burning up at the same time, everything hurt, and I thought I am going to be sick. I just tried to hold it together until I was sure Jacob couldn't see a speck of our car from his place. Then I told Jeff to pull over, he did, and I lost it.

I'm throwing up on the side of the road, in front of brother and cousins. How could this be happening? Just an hour ago, I am loved, happy, considering the situation, and now I'm a potential future murderer. How could he say that, or think that about me? How could he let me walk out the door, out of his life? No goodbye, nothing. I guess it's better to know all this now, and not six months down the road.

Jacob doesn't trust me or believe in me and our future together. I'm crushed emotionally and physically devastated. I love him to the core of my very existence. I will always love him. My heart will always break for the memory of my Jacob.

But our break-up will help Jacob's family treat him better. I'm leaving him knowing that it will make his life better. I guess that is what I can be happy about for now. My Jake, no wait, he's not my Jacob anymore. I don't know how to un-love him? How could he let me leave, just let me go?

Why did he do that, pick the fight, and break my heart? What don't I know? Is he trying to protect me from something? Is it a trust issue? Why can't he be honest with me and tell me what's going on? Include me instead of pushing me away. That's his mistake, a big one. Family roots, they run deep. This isn't over. Somehow love will win out. Granny's last words to me, to us, she said for me to fight. Fight for love Jenna. I may be going home, but this is anything but over.

I'm smart I will figure this out, if there is a way to fix this, I'll do what it takes. I finally discovered what my life can be like to be completely loved and happy. I can't let that joy go, not until I know there is no way for us. But for now, I need to think, pray, and process all of this mess. I need time, I need perspective. I will come up with something, I just have to…

About the Author

Sonny D. Stone was born and raised in the Midwest. She's lived in rural settings in Kansas and Missouri as well as large cities in Louisiana and Minnesota. She enjoys writing, photography, travel, family, friends and pets. She has a great sense of humor and enjoys many styles of music, and a variety of card games, board and video games and sports. Sonny wanted to share a story of romance and mystery. She had a blast writing this trilogy taking readers on travels with twists and unexpected turns.

www.ingramcontent.com/pod-product-compliance
Lightning Source LLC
Chambersburg PA
CBHW061143170626
46809CB00003B/972